I0597435

DANNY ORLIS
AND THE
TIME OF TESTING

DANNY ORLIS
AND THE
TIME OF TESTING

BERNARD PALMER

Please note that several books in the Danny Orlis series are published by Sword of the Lord Publications and are available for purchase on their website, www.swordbooks.com.

Danny Orlis and the Time of Testing
© 2023 by Bernard Palmer
All rights reserved. First edition 1961.
Second edition 2024.

Please do not reproduce, store in a retrieval system, or transmit in any form or by any means – electronic, mechanical, photocopying, recording, or otherwise, without written permission from the publisher.

Scripture quotations from The Authorized (King James) Version. Rights in the Authorized Version in the United Kingdom are vested in the Crown. Reproduced by permission of the Crown's patentee, Cambridge University Press.

Cover Artwork: Larry Lecheler
Editor: Jon D. Fogdall

Aneko Press *Youth*

www.anekopress.com

Aneko Press, Life Sentence Publishing, and our logos are trademarks of Life Sentence Publishing, Inc.
203 E. Birch Street
P.O. Box 652
Abbotsford, WI 54405

JUVENILE FICTION / Religious / Christian / Action & Adventure

Paperback ISBN: 978-1-62245-996-4

eBook ISBN: 978-1-62245-997-1

10   9   8   7   6   5   4   3   2   1

Available where books are sold

CONTENTS

CHAPTER 1

EMERGENCY CALL

Danny Orlis wiped the perspiration from his forehead and sat down on a straight-backed chair. The Guatemala sun was scorching the little coastal jungle compound where he and Kay were living.

"How do you feel, Danny?" Kay asked.

"I'll be all right," he told her, "as soon as we get that runway finished."

"You've been working so long on it."

"You're telling me," he grinned. "It really doesn't look like it would be such a big job to make a clearing to land a small plane, but in this heat it's rugged. I wonder if we'll ever get it finished."

She went to the refrigerator and poured a glass of cold water for him.

"When do you take another flying lesson, Danny?"

"I was supposed to go tomorrow," he answered,

"but Johnny had to have his plane engine overhauled and he won't be able to fly for a week or so."

He sighed deeply.

"Maybe by that time we can have the runway finished and I won't have to make that 30-mile trip by dugout anymore."

He drank the water slowly.

"The time we have to spend getting from one place to another bothers me a great deal, Kay," he continued. "I can't feel that we're using the Lord's time or His servants wisely. There are thousands and thousands of people in this area who have never heard that Jesus Christ died for their sins. And how do we spend most of our time? Poling a flimsy dugout up the river to reach them, or cutting heavy jungle growth with an ax. What I wouldn't give for a couple of good bulldozers for about a day!"

"I know, darling," she replied. "But even I can remember when it was much slower and more difficult than now. Before Daddy was killed, he used to walk through the mountains from one village to another. He was often gone from home several weeks at a time."

She poured him another glass of water and sat down across from him. Her face was full of concern.

"Danny," she spoke suddenly, "you promised me you were going to take it a little easier. You shouldn't be working so hard in this heat."

"Look who's talking," he said grinning. "You've been going some fifteen hours a day yourself."

"But I'm not out in the hot sun."

Kay leaned forward.

"You know how dangerous sunstroke is, Danny. You will be careful, won't you?"

"Of course I will."

She wiped at her forehead wearily.

"Why don't you take a few days off and we'll go somewhere for a short rest?"

He shook his head.

"No can do now. The plane will be coming down before long." He put his arm around her shoulder. "I want to have that runway finished so it can land right in our front yard."

"Then there will be landing strips at the villages we serve," she reminded him. "You'll have to help with that."

"Some of them already are underway," he answered. "And when we start landing to take out their sick and bring them the story of Christ, you can be sure the others will get strips cleared soon enough."

He smiled.

"It's hard now, Kay, but once we get things running smoothly we'll be able to stop for a little rest."

She shook her head in despair.

"If I know you," she said, "by that time you'll have six other projects under way that'll have to be done."

* * *

The next morning Danny went back to the landing strip with the other men. Kay stood in the doorway of their little hut and watched him leave. For the first time since they had come to Guatemala, she would have preferred to keep him at home.

She spent half an hour or so studying her Bible before going over to the hospital. She had just finished praying when she heard an excited voice outside.

"*Señora!*"

She straightened suddenly.

"*Señora!* Hurry! Open the door!"

Kay Orlis opened the door to see a squat Indian with a deeply concerned look on his face standing before her.

"What is it?" she asked in Spanish. "What's wrong?"

"It is my son!" the man said. "He is much sick! I come for the *señor* to have him get the white man of medicine. Our own medicine man, he do no good."

"The *señor* is away now," Kay explained, "but we will get help for your son. What is the nature of his illness?"

The man seemed not to understand. He gestured with his hands.

"He very sick. Very sick. You come to village!"

With that the Indian turned and trotted into the brush. Kay was so startled by his sudden appearance and departure that she stood motionless as she watched him disappear.

"I don't even know where his son is!" she exclaimed aloud. Then she realized this was the same man she and Danny had seen at their services up the river. He lived in the first village.

She got her things together quickly and went over to the dispensary for Patty Jenkins, a registered nurse.

"Should we take along an interpreter?" Patty asked. "You know how creaky my Spanish is, and I'm just starting to learn the tribal language."

"I'll go and interpret for you."

"You have other things to do," the nurse told her. "I can manage."

"But I have to go," Kay repeated. "You see, this man came to Danny and me because he has come to think of us as his friends. He'll be at that hut when we get there. If neither Danny nor I are with you, he'll think we only pretend to be friendly and don't mean it at all."

The nurse got her bag, and she and Kay hurried down to the river to Danny's dugout.

"I'm amazed at all the things we must learn about the customs and the culture of these people," she said. "Sometimes it frightens me."

"It shouldn't," Kay answered. "It won't be long until you'll become so accustomed to those things, you'll observe them without actually realizing it."

At the river they paused momentarily.

"I was going to ask the man who came for help if he'd pole our dugout upstream for us," she continued, "but he got away before I could talk to him."

"That's something I can learn, I guess," Patty remarked as she helped Kay push the long, slender dugout canoe into the sluggish river.

The perspiration stood out on their faces and coursed down their cheeks.

"Have you ever poled a dugout, Patty?" Kay asked her companion as she stepped quickly into the narrow craft and deftly picked up the long pole.

"I've been in a canoe a few times since I've been down here, and I've tried to pole a time or two, but I haven't been able to get the hang of it."

"I'll take it for a while," Kay said.

She began to pole the clumsy craft upstream.

The current seemed sluggish, but it was a powerful force to be overcome. Kay shoved the pole down into the mud and pushed against it. The dugout moved forward slowly. She lifted the pole, drew it forward, and plunged it to the bottom once more. Again and again and again she repeated the motion rhythmically, until her muscles throbbed and perspiration ran down into her eyes.

"You can't keep that up, Kay," Patty protested. "Give me the pole. I'm going to take my turn."

"This isn't too hard," Kay said. "I've done it lots of times. Besides, we'll be there in just a little while."

"I can learn," Patty insisted.

She took the pole and tried her best to handle it. But there was no time for Kay to show her how. She floundered with it and almost fell in, although poling looked deceptively simple.

"Let me have it, Patty," Kay spoke up. "It takes quite a little time to learn how to pole effectively.

Until you do learn it you probably won't be able to make much progress."

Patty handed the pole back to Kay and sat down.

"I feel like a heel not being able to help you."

"You'll have your share of poling dugouts," Kay went on. And then she remembered the landing strip and the plane that was coming from the States. "Or, maybe you won't."

It seemed to Kay that they would never reach the little village. She worked so hard her back throbbed with pain and her breath came in short gasps. She tried to keep the dugout in the shade as they labored upstream, but that was only possible a few minutes at a time. And the sun bore down on them relentlessly. It was now the time of day that activity came to a halt and most people in the area crawled into their hammocks to rest. Yet she and Patty could not stop.

"How much farther is it?" the nurse asked at last.

"I thought we'd be there by this time," Kay replied.

She stopped for a moment or two, leaning on the pole and breathing heavily.

It didn't seem as though she could possibly lift the heavy pole again. But she had to lift it. Lift it, drag it forward, and thrust it to the bottom in a slow but steady rhythm.

Silently she prayed for strength.

The minutes dragged on as hours, and still the hopeless tangle of jungle looked unchanged, untouched by human hands. At last, they rounded a sharp bend and Patty cried out excitedly.

"There it is, Kay!"

Kay stopped poling momentarily.

"Thank You, God!" she whispered.

In another minute or two, the canoe reached shore and a group of natives came down to meet them.

"You have come for to help Pietro?" a boy of twelve or fourteen asked.

"They are only women," the men muttered darkly among themselves. "What can they know of powerful medicine?"

"Come," the boy said, "I take you to Pietro."

The men were still shaking their heads.

Kay and Patty, however, only vaguely sensed their disapproval as they hurried along the trail with their guide until at last they came to a tiny hut that stood alone among the trees. A frail, gray-haired Indian woman came out to meet them.

"You have come," she said thankfully in her native tongue to Kay. "You have come."

"Ask her where the patient is?" Patty put in anxiously, "and if we can see him."

"He's in the hut," Kay whispered. "She'll take us to him."

The woman motioned for them to go into the little hut. They did so, ducking under the narrow doorway. There, on a pile of rags in one corner, lay a boy of about eighteen. His face was sallow, and his eyes were dull.

Patty placed a hand on his forehead.

"He's burning with fever. Hand me the thermometer from the bag, please."

She took his temperature, noted it in her book, and asked a few questions through Kay.

"I'm confident it's pneumonia," Patty said, "but I wish there was a good doctor here to give me orders."

"We've been praying for one," Kay remarked simply. "Until then we've got to do the best we can."

Patty listened to the boy's breathing once more.

"It's pneumonia. It's got to be."

"And pneumonia is serious enough without anti-biotics," Kay put in.

"I have a little penicillin," Patty said.

She took a sterile hypodermic needle and gave the boy an injection. Then she handed his mother a few tablets and gave her careful instructions about giving them to her sick son.

When Kay finished interpreting, the woman took her hand between her own scrawny fingers and squeezed them tightly.

"Oh, thank you," she spoke in poor Spanish. "Thank you."

"We have come in the name of Jesus," Kay spoke in the woman's own language. "Have you ever heard the story of Jesus?"

A perplexed look came to the woman's face.

"One time I go to the service with my husband," she said, "when you come to the village. But I do not understand."

Kay sat down with her and patiently went over the steps of salvation, one by one. There was interest, but the woman kept glancing over her shoulder at the little hut behind them.

"We will come back and talk with you again," the young missionary said smiling, "when Pietro is better."

"Sí," she replied, reverting to Spanish once more, "when Pietro is better."

Finally, they left the little hut and walked back toward the village where they had left the dugout canoe. Their guide started as rapidly as before, but after a short distance Kay stopped him.

"I'll have to go a little slower," she explained. "I can't walk so fast."

Patty turned toward her quickly.

Kay's face was white and drawn, and suddenly she looked very, very tired.

"Kay!" she exclaimed. "Are you all right?"

CHAPTER 2

IN THE JUNGLE

I–I'm all right," Kay replied.

Her voice quavered slightly.

"You'd better sit down for a few minutes," Patty told her.

She led Kay to a grassy knoll and had her sit down in the shade of a big tree. The heat seemed to close in about them until their breathing was labored.

"Don't be so concerned about me," Kay protested, wiping the perspiration from her forehead. "I'll be all right. It's just that we were walking so fast that I'm a little out of breath."

The nurse took her pulse before replying.

"Your pulse is almost normal," she said. "I'm thankful for that. But I think we'd better stay here for a while and rest. Heat exhaustion is nothing to fool with."

"I've never thought it was so bad," Kay replied.

"That's probably because you've never seen a

serious case of it," the nurse went on. "And heat stroke, which is something different but is caused in much the same way, is almost always fatal."

Kay shook her head.

"I guess I've known that, but somehow you think of heat stroke as the sort of thing that happens to someone else."

They sat for fifteen or twenty minutes in the shade along the trail. And when they started once more, Patty insisted that they go at a more leisurely pace.

"And," she said as they neared the village, "I think we'd better get someone to pole the dugout back to the compound for us. I don't know enough about it, and I don't like the idea of your doing it, Kay. That weak spell you had back there disturbs me."

"That was nothing," Kay insisted. "I feel as well as ever. I think I was just tired."

"Just the same I don't want you to pole that canoe if we can find someone else to do it."

When they reached the village, Kay turned to their guide and asked about someone to take them downstream to the mission compound.

"Tomorrow," he said, "we can get someone to take you there."

"But we must go tonight."

A strange, haunted look came into the boy's eyes.

"Oh, no!" he exclaimed, looking about wildly as though troubled by the very thought. "No one will go tonight. Tomorrow. Early tomorrow morning."

She shook her head.

"We must go tonight."

For a long minute he stared at her. Then, without speaking a word, he turned and fled into the jungle.

"Now what do you make of that?" Patty wanted to know.

"He just didn't want to take us down to the compound this evening," Kay answered.

"But why? He was so friendly until you told him we wanted to go this evening. Then his whole attitude changed."

Kay nodded.

"It's just another place where the superstition that rules these poor people shows through. They have so many demons and evil spirits they're afraid of that they don't dare to go out of their villages at night. And they won't go out if they can possibly get out of it."

Patty was silent for a minute or two.

"And one of the doctors I used to work with said he couldn't understand why we wanted to come down here and try to change these people," she mused. "He contended that they're happy enough with their own religion."

"I'm afraid there are some Christian people who come close to having that same opinion," Kay told her, "At least as far as their actions toward supporting missions and missionaries are concerned."

She turned toward the river.

"I think we should start home now, Patty," she

went on. "Danny's going to be worried if we aren't there by the time he and the others get off work."

"Are you sure you feel all right?"

"I feel fine now."

They got the canoe into the river again and Kay took the pole. The current, that seemed deceptively slow and sluggish, was actually very powerful. And the river looped and twisted through the jungle like a gigantic, writhing snake. It was all Kay could do to keep the nose of the unwieldy craft headed into the middle of the stream. Two or three times they rammed ashore on a sharp curve, and it was all both of them could do to push the dugout backward and get it moving once more.

Kay felt the perspiration soaking her clothes.

They had been gone from the village for an hour or so when suddenly, without warning, it happened.

Kay's eyes blurred. Her head swam, and for an instant she thought she was going to faint. She clung tightly to the pole and leaned against it for support.

Patty saw the color go out of her cheeks and her knees sag.

"Kay!" she cried excitedly. "Kay! What's wrong?"

Kay tried to speak, but she could not. Her trembling lips parted, her eyes glazed, and she crumpled slowly to the bottom of the canoe.

"Kay!" the young nurse cried. "Kay! What's the matter?"

The current whipped the canoe ashore and held it broadside against the mud bank.

Patty crept back to the place where Kay had fallen. Kay's pulse was weak and fluttering and her head was hot to the touch. The nurse's own heart was hammering furiously.

"Heat exhaustion!" she exclaimed under her breath, as she struggled to get Kay ashore.

Moisture beaded the unconscious girl's face, Patty noted thankfully. That meant she hadn't quite gone into heat stroke.

Hurriedly, Patty moistened strips of cloth torn from her light jacket and placed them on Kay's forehead.

After the first shock was over, the young nurse began to work calmly and efficiently. She saw that Kay would be lying in the rays of the sun in a few moments and moved her to a location where the shade was deeper, Then she began to wipe Kay's face with her wet handkerchief, praying silently all the while.

A great dread swept over Patty.

What would she do if Kay didn't come to? What would she do if the sick girl got worse? How would–? Grimly she forced such thoughts from her mind.

She changed the wet compresses on Kay's forehead regularly and took her rapid pulse.

At last Kay stirred, fitfully.

"Kay," Patty spoke in a soft voice. "Kay."

The stricken girl opened her eyes briefly and looked about.

"Patty," she asked, "what happened? I–"

"Just relax," Patty told her, striving to sound calm

and confident. "Everything's going to be all right now. You just got a little too much sun."

She closed her eyes for a time.

"I–I feel so weak," Kay went on. "I can't understand it."

She expelled her breath slowly.

"Don't try to talk."

"But I felt all right until just a minute ago," she said. "Until I got the most peculiar feeling. I've never had anything like it. I knew I was going to collapse and there wasn't a thing I could do about it."

"You fainted," the nurse said.

There was a long silence.

"Where are we?" Kay asked at last.

Patty ventured a smile.

"I don't really know," she replied. "We're on the riverbank somewhere between the village and the mission compound. I don't dare try to take you downstream in the dugout. I'm afraid I'd drown us both."

Kay was silent for a moment.

"But how–how are we going to get home?"

"We may have to wait until morning, or until someone comes after us."

Kay raised up on one elbow quickly. There was panic in her voice.

"But Patty! We can't stay here all night! There's no telling what might happen to us before morning!"

"Now lie down, Kay," the nurse said calmly.

"We've got to put our trust in God. He can take

care of us here on the bank of the river, just as well as He can take care of us back at the compound."

Kay closed her eyes and sighed deeply.

"I'm sorry," she said. "I didn't mean to doubt."

She lay very quietly while Patty got a few dry branches and built a fire.

Darkness was almost upon them.

Somewhere out in the jungle there came the piercing scream of a wild animal!

Patty felt her blood freeze in her veins.

CHAPTER 3

TO THE RESCUE!

Darkness settled over the jungle. And with it the forest seemed to come slowly alive. At first birds began to call one to another through the stillness. Plaintive, musical, and not unpleasant sounds that were reassuring to Patty and Kay, evidence that they were not entirely alone.

But more frightening noises were not long in coming. There was a deep-throated growl that rumbled ominously from a clump of brush at their right – or so it seemed. It was followed closely by a piercing shriek of terror and excited chattering from the trees.

In a moment or two, they could hear the unmistakable noises of animals making their way through the jungle. Some were betrayed only by the gentle rustling of leaves or the stirring of brush or fern. Others crashed with reckless abandon through the forest, disdainful of the fact that the noise betrayed them.

The girls looked at one another uneasily.

"It's strange to be hearing all these noises," Kay said. "I've never thought of the jungle as a noisy place at night until now."

Patty managed a little laugh.

"It sounds like Grand Central Station tonight. I hope those creatures out there know that they are supposed to be afraid of fire."

"Danny says you need never worry about a wild animal attacking as long as you have a good fire."

"Then you can be sure the fire is going to be kept roaring high tonight," the nurse announced.

Patty continued to keep cold compresses on Kay's forehead. The sick girl still had a fever, but it had dropped a degree or two.

For several minutes Patty crouched beside her patient, listening to the sounds of the jungle and shivering involuntarily.

For a long while Kay lay back in silence with her eyes closed. It was such a long time before she spoke again that Patty thought she had dropped off to sleep.

Finally, she opened her eyes a narrow slit.

"Poor Danny. He's going to be terribly worried."

"You left a note telling him where we were going, didn't you?" asked Patty.

Kay shook her head.

"I didn't think we would be gone that long," she replied. "I thought the patient was in the village, and I was sure that we'd be home long before Danny got back from work."

Patty sighed deeply.

"Then there's no way he would know where we are, is there?" she asked. "No way he would know where to look for us?"

"I don't think we told anyone where we were going. Pietro's father was in such a hurry, and I'm afraid I wasn't thinking straight."

The two girls bowed their heads in prayer.

Patty prayed aloud, but Kay lacked the strength to do so. When they finished, she closed her eyes, and in a short while drifted restlessly off to sleep.

* * *

Back at the mission station, Danny Orlis and the others finished work late that afternoon and headed wearily for their homes.

"Another few days like today," Danny said, "and we'll have that landing strip finished. Then I'll be able to take flying lessons right here at home."

"It certainly won't make me feel bad to have this job finished," his companion added. "I don't think we've ever tackled anything more difficult than building this air strip."

"It's this heat," Danny answered. "I don't think the work would be so bad if it weren't for that. The worst of it is we don't get any letup. It just keeps bearing down day after day."

"But when we think of what a plane here on the

station is going to mean to our work," the other missionary continued, "we can stand the discomfort of the heat. Imagine what it will be not to have to depend on those slow, dangerous dugouts, or walking through the jungle to get to our out-stations. Think what it's going to mean to the work here!"

"The pitiful thing as I see it," Danny went on, "is that there hasn't been a plane out here all these years. Think of all the people who might have been reached with the Gospel if there had been. Why this whole area might be transformed!"

By that time, they had reached the little hut where Danny and Kay lived.

"Well, good night," Danny said, turning in at the path to his house. "I'll see you in the morning."

"You'll see me in the morning," his companion replied laughing, "if I can get out of bed. Right now, I'm not sure I'll even be able to get up in the morning."

Danny went to the house and opened the front door.

"Kay!" he called. "Kay."

Only silence greeted him.

He went through the kitchen to the living room, and then to the small bedroom at the back, but she wasn't there.

"Now that's strange," he spoke aloud. "Kay didn't say anything about going somewhere this afternoon, or did she?"

He could not remember.

He left the house and went over to a missionary neighbor.

"Kay isn't around anywhere," he said. "Have you seen her?"

"Isn't she back yet?" Mrs. Benson asked.

"Back yet? I didn't even know she had gone anywhere."

"I saw an Indian go up to your house earlier today," the woman went on. "Someone must have been ill, for Kay went with him and they headed for the dispensary."

"It's strange she didn't leave a note if she was going to be gone very long."

"They left in a hurry," Mrs. Benson continued. "Perhaps it was an emergency and she didn't have time."

"Thanks," Danny said. "I'll go over to the dispensary and see if they know anything about her."

He walked over to the dispensary. It wasn't like Kay to go off that way. It wasn't like her at all. In spite of himself his concern began to grow.

"I'm not at all sure where they went," another missionary said. "But Patty Jenkins went with her, and I think they went up the river. I saw them heading in that direction."

Danny nodded. The station was almost on the ocean, and the only villages on the river were upstream from them.

"How long ago was that?"

"Oh, it's been hours and hours ago. Long before noon. I was sure they would be back before now."

From the dispensary Danny made his way to the

home of Cliff Steams, a missionary about his age, and told him what had taken place.

"Ordinarily, I wouldn't be too concerned about it," Danny concluded, "but Patty hasn't been here very long, and she really doesn't know her way around yet. And practically every time Kay has gone into the jungle I've been along. I'm afraid they may be in some sort of trouble."

"Come on in and have something to eat, Danny," Cliff urged. "If the girls aren't back by the time we've finished, we'll go out and find them."

"That's going to be some job in the dark!"

When they had finished their meal, the two men retraced Danny's steps to the little hut where he and Kay lived. But it was still dark and empty.

"She's not here," Danny said.

"We'd better get a dugout and head upriver," Cliff suggested. "Chances are they've gone to one of the nearby villages. If they'd been going very far, they surely would have gotten one of us to go with them."

"This is just the sort of thing that a plane and a series of landing strips down here would take care of," Danny observed as he and his companion headed for the river. "I could have flown Patty up to any one of a dozen villages and had her back at the dispensary in a couple of hours."

They got a dugout and set out upstream in the pitch blackness of the night. Slowly they felt their way along.

"It's so dark," Cliff Stearns muttered, "that we could probably pass them on the river and never know it."

"It's dark, all right."

Danny breathed deeply and tried to ignore his growing fears.

"I just can't understand Kay going away like this and staying so long without letting me know. It's not like her at all."

"You don't know what happened just before they left," Cliff reminded him. "She probably forgot to write a note, or maybe she thought they would be back before you'd get home from work."

Danny was praying desperately for God's help.

"The girls are probably terrified, wherever they are," he prayed silently. "Be with them, O God, and take care of them and keep them safe."

He and Cliff continued to pole the narrow dugout upstream, methodically, without missing a stroke.

"Wherever they are," Danny said aloud after a time, "I hope they have presence of mind enough to get off the river. This is dangerous enough for anyone who is experienced with a dugout. It could be really rough for them."

Cliff continued to pole without speaking.

Danny did the same.

After what seemed to be an hour or two, they finally rounded a sharp bend and saw a small fire burning in the distance.

Danny stopped poling suddenly and stared anxiously at it.

Cliff Stearns saw it too.

"Do you suppose that could be Kay and Patty?" he wondered; his voice taut.

"I don't know," Danny replied hesitantly. "I don't see how it could be them. What would they be doing ashore at this time of night? If they're anywhere they must be at the village."

When they were almost abreast of the fire Danny stopped poling.

"Listen!" he whispered.

"I can't hear a thing."

There was a brief silence.

"I'm not sure whether I did or not," Danny concluded. "But I think we'd better go ashore and see."

They turned the canoe and began to pole in the direction of the light.

"Hello!" Danny called out.

"Danny!" Patty cried. "Danny!"

"Did you hear that? It's Patty Jenkins!"

"Patty!" Cliff Stearns shouted. "Patty!"

"We're over here!"

Danny noted the fright in her voice.

"Where's Kay?" he demanded. "Is she all right?"

"She's here with me!"

"There's something wrong," Danny said to his companion.

With that he threw his full weight against the pole and the dugout canoe surged toward shore.

"Pole!" Danny shouted. "Pole!"

It seemed to him that the canoe was only creeping forward, but in a surprisingly short time they reached the place where Patty and Kay had stopped.

"Kay!" Danny cried.

Terror gripped him as he saw her lying on the ground. He ran over to her.

"What's wrong?"

He stared at Patty.

"What happened?"

Kay opened her eyes and tried to smile reassuringly, but the faint circle of light from the campfire revealed the pallor in her cheeks.

"I'm all right, Danny," she protested weakly. "I just got a little too much sun, that's all."

He sucked in his breath.

"I should think that's enough."

"But I feel better now," she went on. Her voice was still strained and trembling, though she fought to control it. "I–I got so I couldn't pole the dugout anymore, and we were afraid to go on with Patty poling. So we stopped for the night."

Danny felt her forehead. It was hot to his touch and very dry. He turned to Patty, a question in his eyes. She got to her feet and moved to one side, far enough away so Kay could not hear what was said. Danny followed her.

"How is she?" he asked in a tense whisper.

"Her pulse is rapid, but she seems to be resting easily now. The important thing is to get her temperature down as quickly as possible. I've done what I can, but it's a difficult thing to manage out here."

"Do you think it would be all right to move her?"

"I think it's the only thing to do," she replied. "We've got to get her to the infirmary where we can go to work on that temperature."

Danny walked back to where Kay was lying.

"Well," she said, managing a crooked little grin, "did you and Patty finish your visit?"

"That we did," he answered. "And now we're going to take you for a canoe ride. How does that sound to you?"

"I hope the moon comes up," she answered. "I always like a beautiful moon for my canoe rides."

Danny picked her up and took her down to the dugout. For an instant she clung to him.

"Oh, Danny," she whispered, "I'm so glad you and Cliff came. I was beginning to get terribly frightened."

"Everything's going to be all right now," he assured her.

But in his own heart he wondered.

CHAPTER 4

HAM OPERATORS

Danny Orlis and Cliff Stearns, working hurriedly but efficiently and calmly, pulled the extra dugout far enough on shore to be sure it wouldn't drift away, and the four of them got into the other craft. The two men poled downstream to the mission station.

Danny glanced down at Kay, who had leaned back and closed her eyes. Although he and Cliff worked until the perspiration soaked their shirts and ran in tiny rivulets down their cheeks, and their bodies trembled with exhaustion, it seemed that the canoe only crawled downstream.

But at last, they covered the final hundred yards of the sluggish, twisting river and nosed the canoe ashore.

Danny carried Kay up to the infirmary and the nurses rushed into action. Patty took her temperature while Elva Winton, the night nurse, sent an aid to the other missionaries for ice cubes.

"If it just weren't so hot," Miss Winton put in, "or if we had a small room air conditioner it would help so much."

Danny watched the activity uneasily.

In a few minutes Mr. Hale, the superintendent of the mission, came to the infirmary.

"I just heard what happened, Danny. How is Kay?" He shook his head.

"I was talking with Elva and Patty," the Superintendent said. "They think we should radio for a doctor in Belize. He could fly up to the landing strip where you've been planning to meet the flight instructor."

"But that's some fifteen miles from here," Danny protested. "It would take hours to go up and bring him down here. And if we have to take Kay to the hospital, we could never keep her out in the heat that long to make the trip to the landing strip."

"But we've got to do something."

Danny told Patty that he and Mr. Hale were going to the house to radio for a doctor and went in to see Kay again.

"Now don't worry about me, Danny," she whispered weakly. "I'm going to be all right."

"Sure you are," he told her with a confidence he did not entirely feel. "I'm going over to the house with Mr. Hale for a few minutes. We'll get back as quickly as we can."

She gave him a weak little smile. And almost before he was out the door, she leaned back, exhausted, and closed her eyes.

Over at the Hale house the mission superintendent turned on his short-wave radio transmitter and, picking up the phone, began to call.

"K2LKE stroke TG9 calling V31MHA," he began. "K2LKE stroke TG9 calling V31MHA. Come in, V31MHA. Come in."

There was only the crackling of static.

"He must not be on tonight," Danny muttered. Panic tinged his voice.

Mr. Hale looked at his watch.

"It's getting awfully late, Danny," he said. "We might not be able to arouse anyone."

He turned back to the transmitter.

"This is K2LKE stroke TG9 calling anyone in Belize. This is K2LKE stroke TG9 calling anyone in Belize. Come in, Belize."

The sound of the voice on the receiver startled both of them.

"K2LKE stroke TG9, this is KL7XBN. Come in, preacher. This is Petey."

"You've raised someone!"

"How are you, Petey?" Mr. Hale began. "We've got troubles down here."

"Anything I can help you with?" the ham operator asked.

"If you lived in Belize instead of Anchorage," Mr. Hale told him, "you could help us a great deal. We've got a missionary who is down with heat exhaustion. We've got to get her to a doctor, and get her there fast."

"I talked with D'Arstagon earlier tonight," Petey replied. "He said he was going to a party and wouldn't be on again until tomorrow or the next day."

"Have you talked with anyone else in Belize or near us?" Mr. Hale wanted to know.

"D'Arstagon is the only one I've ever contacted," Petey said. "Sorry."

"If you should contact V31MHA let me know, will you, Pete?" Mr. Hale urged.

"Sure thing," he answered. "I'm sorry to hear about the missionary."

Danny's heart sank.

Another hour passed while Mr. Hale sat at his radio transmitter, trying desperately to raise the ham operator or someone else in Belize.

"I think I'd better go back to the hospital," Danny said at last. "There may be something I can do for Kay."

"I'll keep at this for a time."

When Danny reached the infirmary, he found it quiet. Even Patty had gone to bed.

"She was about exhausted, poor girl," Miss Winton told him. "Today has been quite an ordeal for her, especially since she's a new missionary on the field."

"How is Kay?" Danny asked.

"About the same," the nurse said quietly.

They were still talking when one of the Hale children came hurrying into the building in his pajamas.

"Danny," he cried excitedly, "Dad said for you to send one of the nurses over to our place right away – and hurry."

"But why?" Danny demanded.

"All I know is that Dad came dashing into the bedroom and half jerked me out of bed before I was even awake. He told me to skedaddle over here and have you send a nurse over right away."

"I'll go," Miss Winton said, picking up the bag she used to carry her medicine. "If Kay needs anything, Danny, you call Miss Jenkins. She's sleeping in the next room."

The boy started out of the door with the nurse, but Danny grasped him by the arm.

"What is your dad doing?"

"He was still sitting at the short-wave radio when I left," the boy answered, "but I sure don't know what he was doing. There's nobody up to talk to after midnight."

Danny stared after him. He was tempted to rush back to the Hale house and see what was taking place, but Kay might need him.

He tiptoed into the darkened room where his wife was sleeping. For a long minute he stood there, looking down at her. The soft rays of the full moon filled the room with a mellow light.

Kay's face was flushed with fever and her breath came in short gasps. And there was the slightest trace of perspiration at her hairline and just above her eyebrows. She stirred restlessly, and a groan escaped her lips. Then she lay quiet once more, and he saw that she was still asleep.

Almost without realizing what he was doing, Danny knelt beside her bed and began to pray. He was still on his knees, praying silently, when Miss Winton touched him lightly on the shoulder.

"Kay's asleep now, Danny," she whispered in his ear. "Why don't you try to get a little sleep? I'll wake you if there's the slightest change, or if Kay wakes up."

He followed her out into the corridor.

"What was wrong over at Hale's?" he asked. "Is someone ill?"

"Not at all," she replied. "That ham radio operator who lives in Anchorage, Alaska, got a doctor over to his place. They had me come over to find out how we were treating Kay and to give directions for her care until we can get her to a doctor."

"Thank God," Danny whispered. "Thank God."
"He told us that ordinarily heat exhaustion cases get along quite well after the initial shock," she continued, "providing there's no heart damage or other complications, and assuming that the proper treatment is given."

She paused momentarily.

"Did he tell you how to take care of her?" Danny asked. "Did he tell you what medication to give?"

"Actually," she went on, "the treatment for heat exhaustion without complications is quite simple. He suggested substantially the same treatment that we have been giving. However, he said that if she did not improve almost immediately, he would strongly urge us to get her to a doctor as quickly as possible."

Danny expelled his breath slowly.

"It's reassuring to know that you've been doing what's right for her," he said, "but somehow, I think I'd have felt better if he'd given instructions to use certain medicines, or give shots, or something."

"I know just how you feel, Danny," the nurse went on. "But don't forget that we have access to the most powerful medicine in the world. We can turn to God for help."

Danny went into the waiting room and lay down on a narrow cot. He intended only to close his eyes for a moment or two. But he was so exhausted that he fell asleep immediately, and when he finally awakened the sun was high in the sky and his face and arms were wet with perspiration. He jumped to his feet and hurried down the hall.

Patty Jenkins was coming out of Kay's room.

"How is she?" he demanded, his voice rising.

"She seems to be about the same as last night," Patty answered. "The heat makes it so hard to bring her temperature under control."

Danny squared his shoulders and went into the room. He sat there for fifteen or twenty minutes, talking now and then, or sitting quietly, as Kay indicated interest or lack of it. When she began to doze, he tiptoed out and went to see the superintendent.

"I stayed at my radio until after four this morning," Mr. Hale told him, "and I started in again at seven, but I've not been able to get in touch with D'Arstagon."

"Do you suppose I should try to get to the closest town with a charter plane service," Danny asked, "and get someone to bring a doctor up here?"

"You'd have a 50-mile walk, Danny," Mr. Hale replied. "And in the sort of country you'd have to go through it would take you at least two days, and possibly more."

"But we've got to get someone to help Kay!" Danny exclaimed. "She's got to have a doctor!"

For an instant, a strange look crossed Mr. Hale's face.

"If only we had been able to interest just one young doctor to come down and help us, we wouldn't have any problem."

Then he straightened.

"I'm going back to my radio and see if I can raise someone."

It was shortly after noon when he finally was able to contact the ham operator in Belize.

Quickly Mr. Hale told him of Kay's condition and outlined his problem.

"I will call Dr. Gonzales," D'Arstagon said, "and see what he suggests."

Mr. Hale kept the key open while the ham in Belize phoned the doctor and talked with him.

"The doctor says your patient should be brought down to the hospital as quickly as possible," D'Arstagon repeated. "He said he would be glad to come up with a pilot, but there is so much more he can do in a modern hospital with the proper facilities."

"Can you get a plane to come up?" Mr. Hale asked. "The pilot would have to go fifteen miles or more north of us to find a landing strip long enough to take a light plane, but we will get her up there."

"Do you have any clearing at all?" the ham operator continued. "This friend of mine has a new helio-plane that can land on a yardstick and take off from two, more or less."

"We've got a strip about three-fourths completed," Mr. Hale said, "if that's enough distance."

"How much space do you have?"

The superintendent told him.

"That's more than enough," the radio operator said. "Don't worry about a thing. I'll have the plane up there before you know it."

The hours passed endlessly, but without any sign of the plane. When the sun dipped behind the horizon Danny sought Mr. Hale once more.

"Do you think we should get in touch with Belize again," he asked, "and see if the pilot actually left there? He should have been up here hours ago."

The superintendent was a long while in answering.

"Danny," he said finally, "I just contacted D'Arstagon in Belize. He said the pilot left two hours ago, and he hasn't been able to make radio contact with him since."

CHAPTER 5

AN AIRLIFT

Danny glanced up at the sky. The sun, while not yet set, was already out of sight behind the trees in the west, and the blue of the cloudless sky was turning gray. Nightfall was closing in.

"It's going to be dark in a little while," Danny murmured, trying not to think of the complications that would come with the night. "If he doesn't get here before then–"

"I'll keep trying to make radio contact with him," the superintendent assured him. "I'm sure he'll get in touch with us, or will try to."

Danny was silent for a moment.

"I have it!" he exclaimed suddenly. "We'll light fires along the edge of the landing strip so the pilot will be able to see where to come down when he does find us."

"Good idea, Danny," Mr. Hale agreed. His forehead wrinkled with concern. "Do you want to take care of it, or do you want me to?"

"I'll do it," Danny called over his shoulder. "Cliff will help me."

He almost ran to the Stearns' home for Cliff.

"I'll get a dozen Indians and meet you at the airfield, Danny," his friend told him. "If that pilot is anywhere in the area, we'll make enough light to bring him in."

Danny never did know how the Indians got over to the crude landing strip so quickly. By the time he got there, after stopping at the homes of two more missionaries, Cliff was already on the job with his crew. They swung their machetes furiously and the pile of firewood grew.

"The wood is so green I don't think it will burn very well," Cliff said to Danny some minutes later, "so I sent for some kerosene."

By the time the fires were laid the men arrived with the kerosene. They poured it on the green wood and set it afire. Black smoke curled up about the orange-red flames. As darkness closed in, the fires outlining the landing strip were burning brightly.

Half an hour passed, and Danny and Cliff stood side by side in silence at one end of the clearing.

"That guy must be out of gasoline by this time," Danny concluded finally, giving voice to the dread that had been growing in his heart. "He's already been flying for a long time."

"He must be getting low," Cliff agreed, "but of course we don't know how much gasoline the helioplane carries."

He stopped suddenly.

"Danny!" he exclaimed, his voice growing taut. "Do you hear anything?"

For a moment or two they listened breathlessly.

The only sound was the crackling of burning branches. And then the thin, distant hum grew more apparent.

"Cliff!" Danny cried under his breath. "It's a plane. It's a plane!"

And as they listened, the sound of the motor grew louder and louder. As they stared up into the darkness of the night, the plane came roaring in over the treetops and circled the landing strip. In the darkness, only the tiny lights on the wings and tail and the roar of the engine told them where it was.

Danny watched prayerfully as the lights indicated that the pilot was banking sharply. The wings straightened; then the plane dipped downward so slowly he could scarcely believe it was possible to cut the speed that much and still remain in the air. A moment later the plane was on the ground and rolled to a stop.

Danny and Cliff dashed forward as the pilot opened the cabin door and climbed out.

"Are we glad to see you!" Danny exclaimed. "We'd about given you up for lost."

"I was glad to see those fires, *Señor*," the pilot answered in broken English. "My radio, she conk out on the way. I know it is an emergency from my friend D'Arstagon, so I search and search for you. But–" he shrugged his shoulders expressively, "the darkness, she come. And before I know it, I am lost."

"The men will take care of your plane," Danny told him.

Nevertheless, the pilot waited until he was sure that his craft was securely tied. Once satisfied that everything was in order, he turned with Danny and Cliff, and they walked together toward the mission superintendent's house.

"We were afraid you were almost out of gas," Danny remarked.

"No, *Señor*," the pilot answered. "She have extra wing tanks of petrol for just such an emergency. It was not the petrol, but finding my way back that was the big problem."

He paused significantly.

"The radio, she go out, and then something go wrong with the compass," he continued. "For the first time in my life I have both the compass and the radio go out at the same time. That is one helpless feeling, *señors*. If it had not been for your fires I could have flown until I crashed in the jungle, or the sea, before finding my way to this place. Or maybe, if I had been lucky, I could have found my way back to Belize."

"I–I only wish it were possible for us to take off tonight," Danny told him. "My wife doesn't seem to be getting along as well as she should."

"Tomorrow morning, *Señor*," the pilot said. "We will leave just as soon as she is light."

Danny took the pilot to his little hut, after introducing him to Mr. Hale, and fixed a bed for him in the living room. The following morning, almost before it was light, the young missionary was over at the infirmary to see Kay.

"There is no change," Elva Winton told him.

"We'll be leaving for Belize in a few minutes," Danny informed her. "I wanted to be sure that she would be ready."

Just then the door behind them opened and Mr. Hale came in.

"I've decided to go down to Belize with you," he announced. "I have some business to attend to, and I want to hear what the doctor has to say about Kay."

"I'm certainly glad for that," Danny assured him. "It'll be good to have company. Somehow one feels awfully lonely at a time like this."

They left the infirmary to inform the pilot of their plans.

"I'd like to go along," Mr. Hale said to the pilot. "That is, if you think you can get off the landing strip with the additional weight."

The pilot thought for a moment.

"I think we have plenty of room for the takeoff," he said. "The helioplane is one powerful airplane. It will get us into the air without trouble."

While the pilot idled the motor, Danny and Mr. Hale retraced their steps to the infirmary for Kay.

"I can walk down there," Kay informed them with

some determination. "I'm not so sick that I have to be carried."

"Sick or not," Danny informed her softly, "we're going to carry you. You'll do as we tell you until you're well enough to give the orders."

"All right," she said, putting her arms about his neck and letting him lift her. "But don't say that I didn't warn you. I'm heavier than you think I am."

She was still running a fever, Danny realized as her cheek pressed against his, and her breathing was short and labored.

As soon as they were all in the plane, the pilot took off. In two hours they were at their destination. Mr. Hale had radioed D'Arstagon just before they left, and he had an ambulance waiting at the airport.

"I could just as well have ridden in a car," she protested when she saw it.

"Car nothing," Danny answered, forcing a little laugh. "We want you to go to the hospital in style."

The doctor had her admitted to the hospital and examined her thoroughly. Danny waited in the hall.

"How is she?" he asked Dr. Gonzales when the tall, dark-skinned physician came out of the room.

"She's a very fortunate young woman," he said slowly, "although she is still quite ill. You are probably aware of it, but she was on the verge of heat stroke."

Danny sucked in his breath sharply.

"And is she getting along satisfactorily now?" Mr. Hale put in quickly.

"It is too early to answer a question like that," the doctor replied. "But your nurses have done an excellent job taking care of her. That much we can say.

He took a deep breath.

"She is still running a temperature, although it is somewhat lower than it has been previously, according to the chart your nurse kept."

They walked down the hall to a private consultation room.

"You see," the doctor continued, "the difficulty here in Guatemala is that our climate is working directly against her. This heat is making it more difficult all the time. It keeps her from responding to treatment."

"Isn't there something you can do?" Danny asked anxiously.

"*Sí*" the doctor replied. "We have a number of aids here at the hospital. That is why I asked that she be brought in."

He folded and unfolded his hands as he talked quietly.

"For example," he went on, "we will keep her in an air-conditioned room here at the hospital. That will be of great help to her. But there will be a period of convalescence. The heat will make that period very long and difficult for her."

"Would you suggest a change of climate, doctor?" Mr. Hale put in. "Would it speed her recovery if she were in a place where it didn't get so hot?"

Dr. Gonzales was silent for more than a minute.

"I have always hesitated to make suggestions to

patients that would radically change their lives," he began, "unless I feel there is no other course of action available and I am reasonably sure that a change will provide the answer."

"What about Kay?" Mr. Hale repeated. "Would a more temperate climate help her?"

"If she were one of our people," the doctor said, "I would probably hesitate to tell her what I'm going to tell you gentlemen. There is no question in my mind that the young lady would recover a great deal faster in a cool climate."

He reached over and took a medical book from his desk.

"Here is what the authorities have to say…."

CHAPTER 6

CHANGE OF CLIMATE

Dr. Gonzales had Kay moved to an air-conditioned room immediately and gave detailed instructions for treatment to the nurse on duty. Then he turned back to Danny, noting the weariness in the young man's face.

"And now, young man," he said, "I would suggest that you get some rest. We will see that your wife has everything she needs."

Danny and Mr. Hale walked down to the end of the corridor in silence. Now that Kay was actually in the hospital, a strange emptiness took hold of Danny. And suddenly he was desperately tired.

"What do you think?" he asked after a time.

"I'm thankful she's in Dr. Gonzales' care," Mr. Hale replied. "He impresses me as a very competent physician. And the hospital here is well-equipped. I'm confident she'll be cared for as well here as with your family doctor back home."

Danny sighed deeply.

"I know all that," he said. "And I know that a Christian should turn over things to Christ and not worry. But it's one thing to talk about trusting God in all our troubles, and quite another thing to do it."

"It's times like these," Mr. Hale told him, "that show the depth of a Christian's faith. It's very natural to be concerned. But we must pray continually for strength to leave our problems with Him. God can, and will, take care of Kay. We must trust Him."

Danny nodded.

Neither of them spoke again until they had left the hospital and had entered a small cafe several blocks away.

Across the dinner table Mr. Hale looked up from the menu.

"Danny," he said with a suddenness that startled the young missionary, "there's something I'd like to talk with you about."

He looked up.

"Yes?"

"What did you think of Dr. Gonzales' recommendation?"

"Recommendation?" Danny repeated. "I don't believe I heard any recommendation. I was so concerned about Kay I scarcely heard anything he said."

"About Kay recovering more rapidly if she were convalescing in a cool climate," Mr. Hale went on.

"I heard him say that," Danny replied, "but, to be honest with you, I dismissed it without another thought. Kay and I can't leave now. Furlough time isn't due for a long while."

The waitress came and they gave their orders.

"I'm not talking about furlough now, Danny," the superintendent continued. "As Dr. Gonzales said, heat exhaustion can be serious, and Kay was apparently on the verge of heat stroke."

He paused and looked intently at the young man across from him.

"As you must know, heat stroke is practically always fatal."

Danny winced.

"What would you think of taking Kay home until she recovers from this?"

Danny stared at him incredulously.

"But there's so much to do at the station," Danny protested. "I can't go now. We've almost finished the landing strip, and I'm ready to start my cross-country flying. It won't be long until I'll be able to perform a real service here with the plane. I don't see how I can leave."

Mr. Hale took a moment or two in answering.

"I expected you to think of the work first, Danny," he answered. "You're that sort of a missionary. And I've been very grateful for your energy and devotion. We need more like you. But we cannot be impractical. Kay is young and has a good many years of service ahead of her. We can't jeopardize all of that for an immediate problem."

"I don't know what to say," Danny responded. "I suppose it would be best for Kay to go home for a few weeks. I could stay on here and do what I can alone."

"You don't have to decide now," the superintendent told him. "In fact, I don't suppose it would be wise to come to any decision until we learn definitely how she responds to treatment. The Lord can undertake for her, you know, if it suits His purpose."

"That's what I've been praying for ever since we found her ill in the jungle," Danny replied seriously.

"So have I," Mr. Hale said, "and I know there are many on the compound who are praying for her complete recovery this very minute."

The mission superintendent stayed in Belize for three days before going back to the station. He took care of several matters of business, including the ordering of supplies, before hiring the pilot to fly him back.

Danny went out to the airport with him.

"Remember what I told you, Danny," he said as he got into the cabin of the helioplane. "Pray about this matter and talk with Kay and Dr. Gonzales about it. The doctor will be able to give you advice, and it will be most helpful."

Danny was vaguely disturbed as he watched the powerful motor of the helioplane hurl the sturdy plane into the air with an astonishingly short run on the ground. He and Kay had never been separated a day since they had been married. Now they might be separated for months. He prayed silently as he walked across the terminal to the line of taxicabs.

At the hospital, under the expert care of Dr. Gonzales, Kay responded rapidly to treatment. Yet it was several days before Danny felt it wise to approach her about going to Minnesota for a time. Meanwhile he talked with the doctor about it.

"As I told you," Dr. Gonzales said, "I hesitate to tell anyone to make a move that would seriously disrupt his life. But frankly, if my wife were in the position of your wife, *Señor,* I know that is what I would do."

"But the Lord has called us to serve Him here in Guatemala," Danny protested, "and we're needed desperately on the field."

Dr. Gonzales stared at him.

"I don't know what you mean about the Lord's call," he said, "but I do understand your wife's condition. And I do know that convalescence after heat exhaustion is long and very slow in a place where the heat is as intense as here."

He breathed deeply.

"As you know, the worst season of the year for heat is rapidly approaching. You must think on those things as you make your decision, *Señor.* Much is at stake here."

The day they allowed Kay to sit up, Danny told her what Mr. Hale and Dr. Gonzales had suggested. She listened quietly while he explained their reasoning and gave no sign of concern, except that her hand, resting lightly on his arm, began to tremble slightly.

"I can't go home now, Danny," she said. "Even for a little while. This is where God called us. Actually, we're home now."

"Kay, I know exactly how you feel. God called us here, and you don't see how you can leave the work and the people. I guess I feel pretty much as you do."

"Then it's all settled?"

"There are other things to consider," he continued. "What if your health actually became a hindrance to the other workers on the field? What would happen if you were sick for months and months? What would that do to the ministry here?"

Kay raised her eyes.

"What do you mean?"

"Patty and Elva would probably be spending most of their time taking care of you, rather than doing the work God has called them here to do. And I wouldn't be able to work the way I should either. That would make four missionaries doing a sort of part-time job on the field. Patty, Elva, you, and I." Her eyes sought his.

"You've been praying a lot about this, haven't you, Danny?" She spoke in a tone of voice that showed plainly she knew he had but wanted to be reassured.

"Of course I have."

They bowed their heads and prayed together earnestly.

When Danny got back to his hotel room that night, he had a long letter from Mr. Hale.

"We have been giving prayerful consideration to the matter of Kay and yourself," the superintendent wrote. "Today we had what seems to be an answer to our prayers and evidence of God's leading. Word came from the home office of a young pilot who has been accepted as a missionary candidate and will be coming to our field, at least on a temporary basis. He already has his support and visa.

"That means it will be possible for you to accompany Kay back to the States and get a much-needed rest yourself while she is recuperating. And you can go knowing that the work here will continue to go forward."

The next morning Danny handed Kay the letter and waited in silence while she read it. When she finished, she folded it deliberately and replaced it in the envelope.

"Well," she said, and when she spoke her voice was calm, "it seems that the Lord has settled it for us, doesn't it? And to think that we worried so much about what we should do."

Danny left her room presently and went to a phone booth to call his folks.

"And how is Kay now?" his mother asked.

"She's getting on very well," Danny assured her, "but the doctor says she must get out of this terrific heat for a time. So we'll be going home as soon as she's able to travel."

"I'm very sorry that Kay is ill," Mrs. Orlis told him, "but I don't have to tell you that we'll all be excited at the thought of seeing you both."

"It'll only be for a short time, Mother," Danny said. "We decided to go to Minnesota where it's cool so she could recover faster. That will make it possible for us to get back to work at the mission."

After several days, Dr. Gonzales informed Danny that Kay would soon be able to leave Belize.

"The fact that you are taking her north where it's cool makes it possible for her to leave the hospital much sooner than otherwise," he said.

The following morning Danny flew back to the mission to get the rest of their things.

"And, Danny," Mr. Hale told him, "don't worry about a thing. The important task right now is to get Kay back on her feet again."

"I know," Danny answered, "but I don't have to tell you that it's hard to leave. I almost feel as though I were leaving for good instead of for a few months."

CHAPTER 7

THE FAMILY WELCOME

Danny got back to Belize shortly before dark, and the following morning he and Kay left the hospital to take the airport bus to the terminal on the edge of town.

Kay sat nearest the window, her face silhouetted against the early morning darkness, her hands folded in her lap. Danny looked at her and tried to still the dread in his heart. A dread that overshadowed the regret of leaving their little jungle station.

The doctor had assured him she was getting better, but how could he be sure when she was so pale, weak, and listless, so unlike herself?

He got off of the bus, thankful that the blistering tropical sun was still mercifully hidden, and helped her to the ground.

"Are you sure you don't want me to carry you?" he asked.

She wrinkled her nose at him.

"Danny, I can still walk; I'm not that helpless."

She took a step or two forward and leaned heavily on him for support. Perspiration broke out on her forehead, and he could feel her body trembling.

"Are you all right?"

"I–I didn't realize how weak I was, Danny," she said. "If I can just lean on you, I'll be all right."

He put his arm about her and all but carried her into the air terminal where he found a chair near the gate.

She sat down gratefully.

"You've got a lot of resting to do when we get home, Kay," he said firmly, "and I don't want to hear any talk about you helping with the work. Mother and Roxie will be there to do everything that needs to be done. And if they can't manage, I'll help them."

She smiled.

"You're not going to have to fuss at me about resting, for a while at least. I've never felt quite like I do now. It doesn't seem to matter whether there's any work to do or not. I don't have the ambition for anything."

"And it's a good thing," he answered. "You're going to have to put in double duty resting and taking care of yourself. The sooner you get back on your feet the sooner we'll come back here to work."

The sun was just beginning to chase the darkness away. In the early gray of the morning, they could see their plane being loaded.

"Another half hour," Danny remarked, "and we'll be on our way."

"I'm just beginning to get excited about going back to Minnesota," Kay said. "It's certainly going to be good to see everyone again."

"And the twins and Jim Morgan," Danny added.

"Now that we're actually about to leave, I'm glad we're flying. I'd hate to have to wait for a train or a ship to get us back."

Kay's strength seemed to return as they sat there. She smiled frequently, and the excitement showed in her eyes.

"And I thought I was the only one anxious to get back," she told him.

Danny laughed.

"Remember that country is home to me."

He got to his feet, walked to the gate, and looked out at the plane momentarily, before returning to her.

"I was just thinking about the Lake of the Woods, Kay. The ice will be going out before long if it hasn't gone out already. Did you ever see the breakup?"

She shook her head.

"That's the most beautiful time of year, to my way of thinking. The winter has been long and hard, and by the time spring comes everyone and everything is really weary of it. Then the ice breaks up. Spring comes in like thunder in that country."

"I've heard Dad Orlis talk of it."

"It can be cold and raw and wet, but when the

booming of the breakup starts, as far as most people are concerned, summer has already arrived."

His eyes grew sad.

"It's been years since I've seen that happen."

"If I'm feeling all right, we might be able to go up there, Danny," Kay suggested, "just for a few days."

"I was thinking that myself. We could go up to Pawhasset and fly to the Angle with Tex, just to see how things look around the old place."

Their flight was called, and they started toward the plane slowly. There was never a big crowd boarding the aircraft at Belize and they found seats near the center of the plane.

Kay sighed deeply as it began to roll to the far end of the narrow ribbon of cement.

"You don't know how wonderful it's going to be out of this heat. I've always liked warm weather, but now I just dread to see the sun come up when I know it's going to be so hot."

Danny nodded.

"You've almost got me disliking it."

The plane turned and waited for clearance from the tower.

"I'd feel more at ease about going, Danny, if I knew there was someone who could take over my Bible classes while we're gone."

"I talked with Mr. Hale about it before I left the mission yesterday. He said they had a meeting and worked out a plan to share the work you and I have been doing. Except for the flying, that is. And the new pilot will be taking over that chore as soon as the landing strip is completed."

A smile returned to her face.

"I'm thankful for that. It's hard enough leaving. It would be terrible to think that our going would hinder the work."

* * *

Back in Cedarton, Minnesota, the Orlis family was up an hour earlier than usual and had already finished breakfast. Excitement electrified the little group at the table.

"Just think," Ron said, "tonight Danny and Kay will be home with us. I still can scarcely believe it."

"I don't know whether I'm going to be able to study today or not," Roxie put in. "It's going to be wonderful to see them."

Mrs. Orlis frowned.

"If only Kay were well," she said with concern in her voice. "She must be quite ill, or they would never decide it was necessary to leave the field, even for a little while. Every letter they've written is full of talk about all the work they have to do."

"Now, Mother," her husband chided gently, "let's be thankful they're coming home to visit us for a while, and trust God to take care of her."

He reached over and affectionately patted his wife on the arm.

"I'm sorry, Carl. I know I shouldn't worry, but there are times when it's hard not to."

He nodded understandingly.

For a time, no one spoke.

"I'm like Roxie," Jim Morgan broke in at last. "I'm going to find it rough to study at school today, knowing that Danny and Kay are on their way home."

He paused and glanced at Mr. Orlis to be sure he was listening.

"Fact is," the boy continued, "I just don't see that it would do me any good to go to school today, excited as I am."

Mr. Orlis looked at him and laughed.

"You don't look excited to me," he said jokingly.

Jim scowled.

"I may not look excited on the outside," he answered, "but I'm sure excited on the inside."

Roxie winked at him.

"It's not going to do you a bit of good," Ron told him. "You're not going to wiggle out of going to school today. You'll have to suffer through it the same as the rest of us."

"It didn't hurt to try, anyway."

Ron turned to his dad.

"What time does the plane come into Minneapolis?" he asked.

"About 4:45 this afternoon." Mr. Orlis glanced at Jim. "And, Jim, I think it's enough of an occasion for all of us to go down to the airport and meet them."

"Oh, boy!" Jim exclaimed.

"Oh, Daddy," Roxie cried, "that will be super."

"We won't have to leave here until noon," Mr. Orlis went on. "We'll send an excuse with you, that is if you'd like to go with us."

"If I'd like to?" he echoed. "Of course!"

That afternoon they all rode down to Minneapolis St. Paul International Airport to meet Danny and Kay.

"I didn't think about it before," Jim said looking around, "but our car's about full now. We'll be really packed in here when we pick up Danny and Kay."

"We can always have Roxie sit on your lap," Ron told him impishly.

"Oh, no!" Jim exploded. "No, sir! No girl's going to sit on my lap!"

"Don't get so mad at me," Roxie responded, laughing good-naturedly. "It wasn't my idea."

After an hour or so, Mrs. Orlis looked at her watch.

"We're not going to have to wait very long for the plane," she said. "It's 3:30 now, and we've got to drive all around the city."

"To tell you the truth, it's taken a little longer to drive down here than I thought it would," Mr. Orlis replied.

As they pulled into the parking lot at the big airport that served both Minneapolis and St. Paul, a huge airliner came gliding down.

"Do you suppose that's the plane they're on?" Ron asked tensely, getting out of the car and starting toward the terminal.

"It could be," Mr. Orlis answered.

By the time they reached the waiting room the passengers were coming through the gate at the far end of the terminal.

Ron spied his tall, muscular brother almost immediately.

"Danny!" he called out, starting for him on the run. "Danny!"

Danny and Kay were walking slowly toward them.

Mrs. Orlis caught her breath when she saw her daughter-in-law.

"Oh, Carl," she whispered in dismay, "look how pale and weak Kay is!"

CHAPTER 8

PRAYER ANSWERED

The Orlis family stood for a moment or two in an excited little group about Danny and Kay. Everyone was talking at once.

"It's sure great to be home!" Danny exclaimed. "And it's really great to see all of you again!"

He looked at Ron appraisingly.

"What are you trying to do? Get bigger than I am?"

Roxie went over to where Kay and Mrs. Orlis were standing.

"How do you feel, Kay?" she asked.

The girl managed to give a little smile of reassurance.

"I feel all right now, except that I get sort of tired."

"Are you sure you feel all right?" Mrs. Orlis wanted to know.

"That cooking of yours will soon put a little weight on her, Mom," Danny interrupted.

"I think I feel better already," Kay volunteered.

She paused for a moment. "You have no idea how good it is to have it cool. I know I'm going to get a lot better, and very fast."

"Right now, I think you'd better get to the car," Danny told her. "Ron and I will get the bags."

"I'll help you," Jim volunteered.

Danny reached over and rumpled the boy's hair.

The three of them went to pick up the luggage, while the rest of the family walked slowly back to the old car the Foresters had loaned them. In a moment or two the boys were back, and they all crowded in. Danny got behind the wheel and headed for I-494, that looped the Twin Cities, and then headed north.

Almost as soon as the car started to move, Kay leaned back in the seat and closed her eyes. Mrs. Orlis noticed it and signaled the others to be quiet. In a few minutes, the girl drifted off to sleep. They were halfway to Cedarton before she awakened.

She looked at Danny accusingly.

"Danny Orlis! Why did you let me sleep that way? I didn't want to miss out on anything."

"You needed the rest," he told her. "And besides, we had to have some time to talk about you."

"You're going to have to tell me every single thing that's been said when we get home," she countered good-naturedly. "I don't want to miss a word."

They stopped in a little cafe and had dinner now that Kay was awake, before driving the rest of the way to Cedarton.

"Dr. Nielsen said he would like you to come out to the school, Danny," Ron told his older brother. "I think he wants to make arrangements for you to speak about Missions at a chapel service."

Danny nodded.

"I'd like that," he said. "There are some things you learn on the mission field that you wish you'd known when you were still at school. I'd like to share some of those things with the kids."

"And, Kay," Roxie added, "they'd like to have you speak too, as soon as you're strong enough."

They drove into Cedarton and across town to the Forester home.

"We're back," Kay said, breathing deeply. "Oh, but it's good to be here!"

"I think you'd better go up to bed," Danny told her. "This has been a long, hard day."

She did not protest.

"You'll be up in a little while, won't you?"

"Just as soon as I've had a chance to visit with Mother and Dad for a while."

She went upstairs slowly, as though it took all her strength.

"I called the Forester's family doctor and talked with him about Kay this morning," Mr. Orlis said when she was gone. "He thinks it would be wise for her to see him in a few days as soon as she's rested from the trip. He wants to examine her thoroughly."

"That's fine, Dad," Danny replied. "I have her file

that Dr. Gonzales kept. He suggested that we get Kay in the hands of a good physician as soon as possible and give him the file so he'll know everything about her condition and what medication has been given."

"Just what did he say about her condition, Danny?" Mrs. Orlis asked, her voice still tinged with concern.

"He seemed to think she's making satisfactory progress. Of course, he said she should be watched closely for a time and should get a great deal of rest. He was very anxious that we get her out of that stifling hot climate."

"It certainly seems like old times to have you back home, Danny," Mr. Orlis continued, changing the subject after Mrs. Orlis asked a few more questions.

"You can say that again."

"You and I will have to get up to the Angle and do a little fishing before you and Kay go back."

"Sounds like a good idea. I've done a lot of fishing; since we left the Angle, but somehow it never seems quite the same as it does up there."

The next day Danny and Kay decided to see the doctor. He examined her carefully and prescribed plenty of rest.

"I think you'll find a marked improvement in the way you feel, Mrs. Orlis," the doctor said, "now that you're in a cool climate. In many of these heat exhaustion cases that seems to be a determining factor."

"I've been trying to make myself believe that I feel a little better already," Kay answered. "But to be honest with you, I'm not sure whether it's the natural excitement of being back home, or because we're in a place where it isn't so hot."

The doctor smiled.

"It's probably a little of both," he replied, taking a prescription pad and scribbling on it hurriedly. "Get this prescription filled and take the medicine according to directions. Get plenty of rest and come to see me next week."

When they were outside Danny turned to his young wife.

"You know, Kay," he began, "I'm very encouraged by the way you're responding. I don't think it's going to be too long until we'll be able to go back to the field."

They crossed the street and got into the car.

"With all the prayer that is going up, I should be feeling better," she said confidently. "I know it isn't going to be too long until I'm completely well."

As the days passed, Kay could feel her strength returning. Danny and the others noticed it too. She got up a little earlier each morning, walked with more life, and carried on more animated conversations. She laughed often.

But the days began to drag with increasing heaviness for Danny.

"I'm not used to sitting around this way, Dad," he complained one evening. "I've gone out on a few speaking engagements, but I'm not satisfied with that. I've got to have something to do. I've got to go to work."

Mr. Orlis put aside his newspaper.

"There's not a great deal of work around a town like Cedarton at this time of year," he reminded him. "Things actually don't start to open up until the tourists begin to come in."

"I've found that out," Danny replied. "I was out trying to get a job this morning – any kind of a job that would let me make a little money. But I didn't have any success."

"You have your missionary support. That's still going on."

"I know that, but there are some things I'd like to take back to Guatemala. A movie projector and a small generator, for one thing, so we could show films to our people. And some small radios they could use to pick up Gospel broadcasts in their homes."

"You might be able to have those things anyway," Mr. Orlis said, "by the time you go back."

"Even if I didn't need the money, I wouldn't want to hang around anymore. A guy my age has to have something to do."

"It's too bad you can't continue your flying lessons," his dad remarked. "It would be so much easier here than down in Guatemala."

Danny frowned momentarily. Then his eyes lit.

"That would be something I could do to keep my time occupied and still be accomplishing something."

"There's a guy here in Cedarton who is teaching students to fly. I don't know what he charges, but it should be in line with what it costs other places," offered his father.

"I think maybe I'll get in touch with Tex," Danny said. "He's always been a good friend of mine, and he's done a lot of the same sort of flying I'd be doing in Guatemala. He might have time to take me on."

His father nodded.

"He's careful too. That's important, I think."

That evening Danny wrote a letter to the veteran bush pilot who lived near Baudette, Minnesota. An answer came within a week. He tore open the letter and read it hurriedly.

Kay, who had been watching from across the room, read the answer in his face.

"He'll take you on as a student, won't he?" she asked.

He nodded.

"Just listen to this. 'I'd consider it a real privilege to help you with your flying, Danny. It would mean a little extra expense for you and Kay, but if you could come up here and stay for a time you could go with me on my regular runs. You would be getting your experience, and a lot of cross-country flying which would be invaluable, and I wouldn't have to charge you anything for the lessons.'"

"Oh, Danny!" Kay exclaimed. "That's wonderful!"

"It's an answer to prayer, honey," her young husband said fervently. "That's what it is. An answer to prayer.

CHAPTER 9

HOUSE HUNTING

Time seemed to pass swiftly, and Kay appeared to be getting better with each passing day. She was able to go to church and prayer meetings regularly, and insisted on helping Mrs. Orlis and Roxie with the housework.

"I've got to do something to regain my strength," she countered, in answer to their protests. "And besides, the doctor tells me I'm making excellent progress. I really feel better doing something than lying around all the time."

Danny's impatience to get up with Tex continued to grow.

"We've got to get up there before long, Kay," he said, "and get on with those flying lessons. I want to have all of that out of the way by the time we're ready to go back to the field."

"I'm ready any time," Kay responded. "You'll have

to hurry with those flying lessons too. If you don't, I'll be ready to go back before you will."

Mrs. Orlis came to the dining room door and looked in on them.

"I couldn't help hearing what you've been saying," she said. "I don't want to interfere, but do you think you're ready to leave the doctor's care, Kay?"

"Didn't we tell you, Mother Orlis?" Kay asked. "I don't have to go back to the doctor for another month. Isn't that wonderful?"

Mrs. Orlis' eyes revealed her relief.

"That is good news."

She turned to Danny.

"But you still don't want to be in too big a hurry about going back to Guatemala. The doctor is going to insist that Kay is in first-class physical condition before he releases her."

"He won't insist on it any more than I will," Danny asserted firmly. "The climate in Guatemala is hard enough on a person who is entirely well. Kay would be down sick again in no time if we should go back before she's physically fit. And that wouldn't help anyone."

Mr. Orlis passed them and went out on the porch where he stood in silence, looking about. Danny left his mother and Kay still talking and sauntered out to join his dad. He leaned languidly against the porch railing.

It was a warm May afternoon. The sun ruled the cloudless sky with a gentle hand, caressing the green lawns and beckoning the bordering flowers and the raspberry bushes to burst into bloom. The wind, little more than a whisper, was tenderly moving the tiny new leaves. Boys on the way home from school were talking excitedly of baseball, and the girls were playing hopscotch on the walk.

"Does all this make you wish we were back on the Angle, Danny?" Mr. Orlis asked.

"You can say that again, Dad."

Danny smiled.

"You know, this is the sort of day I used to dream about when we were in Guatemala. The weather down there is warm and all that, but we don't have anything as breathtaking as this. The plants don't awaken all at once, the way they do here. In the tropics one plant blooms while another rests. The change is so gradual a person actually never notices it."

"I suppose that's why spring is the favorite time of the year for so many of us northerners," Mr. Orlis continued. "Spring seems to explode on us. And when that happens, we know it's not long until summer."

Danny moved to the steps and sat down. Then his dad sat down nearby.

"We really should be back home before long," he went on. "There's a lot of work to do opening the place after having it closed all winter, and getting the cabins ready for the fishermen. It won't be long until they'll start coming. We've already had a few reservations."

"Now, Dad," Danny broke in, "don't start worrying about the work you've got to do at home. Kay and I have been talking about that. We've already decided that we're going up to help you get things in shape. And Ron says that he and Roxie and Jim want to help too. With all of us working it won't take very long to get the whole place in good order."

"You and Kay don't have time to go up there and take care of our work," Mr. Orlis protested. "You've got things of your own to do."

"We don't have anything to do that's more important than helping you and Mother," Danny answered. "You've spent your whole lives helping others. Now it's time that you get a little help for a change."

Mr. Orlis laughed.

"We're not quite helpless yet."

But there was real relief in his voice.

"No, you're not helpless," Danny told him. "And we're going to do what we can to help you stay as you are. We can't let you go back up there and work yourselves sick. It just isn't worth it."

The next day Danny and Kay got in the used car Danny had bought to get around in while they were home and drove up to Pawhasset, the little Lake of the Woods community, where they were going to live for a time.

The weather that morning was a duplicate of what it had been every day for a week. The grass was green and bright new leaves were bursting out of swelling buds. Even the evergreens seemed greener. Kay leaned back against the cushion and looked about, feasting on the fresh new beauty of the forests and meadows.

"Oh, Danny," she exclaimed happily, "isn't it beautiful up here?"

"It's the most beautiful place I've ever been," he told her. "That's for sure."

"That's just the way I feel. It seems to get more beautiful each mile we go north."

"You sound like a real northerner to me. I believe the country's gotten into your blood too."

"It's catching," Kay answered. "I got it from being married to you."

His face grew pensive.

"There are times when I think I'd like nothing more than to be living back on the Angle."

"Don't say that, Danny!" Kay protested quickly. "Don't even think it! Our place is back on the mission field. We can't even consider staying here."

"I know that," he replied softly. "I guess I was just dreaming out loud. Coming back here, as much as I would like it, could never take the place of Guatemala. I'm sure you know that."

He breathed deeply.

"I think of the work out there a hundred times a day. I didn't think I'd ever miss the people half as much as I do."

"That's just the way I feel about them," she said. "When I think how long it's been and how much work there is to do out there, I could cry."

Kay was silent for a time. Danny glanced her way now and again, thrilling at the color in her cheeks and at her smile which was natural once more. She was acting more like her old self again. That realization warmed his heart.

In an hour or so they drove into Pawhasset.

"This is a pretty little town, isn't it?" Kay observed, surveying the houses appraisingly.

Danny nodded.

"I've always thought so. It's on Lake of the Woods. I suppose that's one reason I've always been partial to it."

He drove up in front of the town's largest real estate dealer, parked the car, and got out.

"I think the quickest way to see the houses and apartments that are for rent is to stop here. Mr. Blake should have some rental listings if anyone does."

Clyde Blake did have several listings.

"It so happens," he said, "that we've got quite a choice right now. A road construction crew moved out of here a couple of weeks ago and the homes and apartments they lived in are available."

"That's fine," Danny answered. "I told my wife that if anyone would have listings it would be you."

Mr. Blake eyed him quizzically.

"Should I know you?"

"I think so," Danny replied. "My name is Orlis.'"

"Now I know where I've seen you. You live up on the Angle, don't you?"

"That's right. At least I still call the Angle my home, although I haven't been back there to live for quite a while."

"I used to fly up to your place with Tex Williams. I stayed at your folks' place when I went fishing up there."

"I remembered you," Danny said. "That's why we came to you first."

They went out to the car and got in.

"We used to have great times fishing up on the Angle," Mr. Blake went on. "Your dad was a swell guy. A little too religious to suit me, but a swell guy."

The real estate agent drove past several houses that were for rent. The first two were big, rambling places that were almost as large as the Forester home in Cedarton and just as nice.

"Either of these places are as fine as anything we have in town," Mr. Blake explained. "The owners have moved away, and you can rent either house with an option to buy, if you like it."

"Oh, we won't be living here long enough to be interested in buying a house," Danny said. "We're planning on going back to the mission field in Guatemala just as soon as possible."

Mr. Blake looked at him but said nothing.

"That's another reason why we want to get something as inexpensive as possible," Kay put in. "We don't have a great deal of money we feel we can put into rent. Anything that is comfortable will do."

The real estate agent turned at the next corner and headed toward the outskirts of the little north woods community.

"I think I have just the house for you," he told

them. "That is, if you don't mind being a little farther out than most places."

"That won't bother us at all," Danny said. "In fact, I think both Kay and I would prefer it."

"This place isn't isolated or anything like that," Mr. Blake continued. "There are neighbors on both sides. But the house is on the edge of town and, frankly, it isn't in the best neighborhood."

"That won't bother us either," Kay replied.

Mr. Blake glanced in her direction.

"Being religious people, I thought you'd be concerned about the sort of neighbors you have," he said.

"We are," she told him significantly, "but the fact that they may not be interested in spiritual things, or even in living clean lives, wouldn't keep us from moving into a house next to them."

He started to speak again but stopped as though uncertain whether to pursue the subject farther or not.

He drove in silence to a small white bungalow set back from the road in a clump of evergreens. There was a big lawn in front and a dozen or more raspberry bushes near the back door. He stopped beside it.

"Now, what do you think of that?"

Kay was the first to speak.

"Why, it's beautiful!" she exclaimed.

"It certainly is," Danny put in.

They got out of the car.

"It is an attractive place at that," Mr. Blake observed. "To tell you the truth I hadn't really noticed it before.

But I do remember that the family who used to live here liked it very much."

His voice was almost drowned by a sudden burst of laughter from the house next door. Danny and Kay both turned quickly. There were half a dozen young guys and girls of high-school age sitting on the porch. Most of them were smoking.

The laughter sounded again, raucously – almost vulgar.

"Wait 'til I tell you the story I heard the other night," one of the boys said loudly, lighting another cigarette. "It's the best story I've heard in a month. This is one that'll make you girls blush."

"You make me blush?" an attractive young brunette countered disdainfully. "Don't be stupid, Brad, boy. I helped write those stories!"

Once more they roared with laughter.

By this time, the youngsters noticed Danny and Kay and Mr. Blake.

"Hurry up with your story, Brad. They want to hear it too."

Danny took Kay by the arm.

"We'd better go inside."

"This sort of thing doesn't happen very often," Mr. Blake apologized, "I can assure you. Mrs. Wheeler works up town and gets home when the stores close. She and her husband aren't like that at all. But you know how young people are these days. They get a little boisterous in their good times."

Danny and Kay glanced at the guys and girls on

the porch. They were younger than Ron and Roxie. Several years younger. And already they were deep in sin. Danny's heart ached for them.

He and Kay went through the little house carefully, opening closets, and noting the size of the rooms. It was an old house. The kitchen had very few built-ins, the plumbing fixtures were old, and a big space heater was in the living room.

"Well," Danny said at last, turning to his young wife, "what do you think?"

"It's a lovely house," she said but there was a note of reluctance in her voice. "It really is."

"For the rent you just can't find anything much better," the real estate man reminded her.

"It's perfectly all right," she repeated. "I wouldn't mind the house at all."

"But you hesitate because of what you heard just now?" Mr. Blake asked. "Is that right?"

"Quite the contrary," Kay said. "As far as I'm concerned that makes the place all the more attractive."

He stared at her, a question in his eyes.

"I don't believe I understand you, Mrs. Orlis," he said. "I can tell by looking at you and talking to you that you find that sort of thing repulsive."

"That's true," she conceded. "Smoking and dirty talk do bother me a great deal. But young people like those need the Savior as well as those who are clean morally."

Her smile came again.

"If we live next to them, we might be able to help them."

Mr. Blake shook his head in disbelief.

CHAPTER 10

NEEDY NEIGHBORS

Danny and Kay supposed they would have to wait until the first of the month to move into the little bungalow, but that did not prove to be necessary.

Clyde Blake wrote to them.

"The owner said that the house is empty now, so you can move in any time you wish, and the rent will start the first of the month."

"What do you think?" Kay asked as Danny read the letter aloud to her. "Do you want to move up to Pawhasset right away, or do you want to wait?"

"It sounds great to me. It means that I can get started with my flying lessons that much sooner." He breathed deeply.

"You know, Kay, I'm ready for my cross-country flights now. All I have to do is spend a little time in the air to get used to flying again and I'll be all set."

Kay crossed the room and sat down.

"I've been thinking about something else, Danny." He nodded.

"Such as those kids on the porch of the house next door?" he asked.

"How did you know?"

"I've been around you for quite a while, Kay," he said. "It's not hard to figure out what you're thinking.

He smiled at her.

"I suppose you've already figured out a way of getting in contact with them."

"I wish I had."

She was very serious.

"As a matter of fact, I've been praying and praying how to make an opening with them, but I don't see any way of managing it. We won't have a thing in common with them."

"Aren't you forgetting something, Kay?" Danny began gently.

"What do you mean?"

"God must have directed us to rent that house. And those kids could well be the reason. If they are, He will provide a way to meet them and to work with them."

She took his hands in hers.

"I know that, Danny. I should never have doubted. But when I see guys and girls like those, who don't know the Savior, my heart aches for them."

The next morning, Danny and Kay planned to go down to the used furniture store in Cedarton to see about getting enough furniture to outfit the little house, but Mrs. Orlis stopped them.

"Since you'll only be there a short time, I thought it would be foolish to invest money in furniture," she said. "So, I've been talking to some of the people in the church. We've been able to find enough to furnish every room in your house. Of course, it won't be the latest style, and maybe the colors won't match too well, but everything we have is serviceable."

Danny and Kay stared at one another.

"Oh, Mother," Kay cried, "that's wonderful!"

"And," Mr. Orlis added, "one of the farmers in the church is willing to haul everything up to Pawhasset in his truck, so it won't cost you a cent to move."

"I've never seen anything like it. I didn't know people could be so kind," Danny exclaimed.

He and his father made arrangements for the farmer to haul the furniture to Pawhasset the following morning.

"I sure hate to think that you're going," Ron said that night as they sat in the living room. "It seems as though you just got here."

"We're not going to be that far away," Danny reminded him. "Especially when you get back on the Angle, Tex and I will be flying in every once in a while."

"And I'll be sneaking a ride every chance I get," Kay put in.

"Now that you're leaving, Danny," Mr. Orlis said, "I don't know whether I'll be able to stand it until school is out. I'm getting awfully eager to get back home."

"Now you know how we've been feeling these past years, Dad," Ron told him. "It's been rough to leave the Angle, and I think I've always felt the worst about this time of year. The trouble is, the days just don't go fast enough."

"Kay and I will go on up and get started with the work the first chance we get," Danny put in. "It's not going to take too long to get things into shape, especially if Jim and Ron and Roxie can help."

Jim's eyes grew bright.

"Just let us know when," he said, "and we'll be there if we have to walk."

* * *

The truck came for the furniture, and Danny and Kay drove up to Pawhasset in their old car.

"I'm so excited about moving into our own home, Danny," Kay said, "that I feel almost guilty about it. I have enjoyed every minute with your folks, but there's nothing like having a place of our own."

"It's strange how often we're thinking the same thing," Danny said. "I wonder if that happens often with other married couples."

Kay snuggled against his shoulder.

"I think I'm almost as excited as I was when we first went down to Guatemala."

They were at Pawhasset before noon, and by 3 o'clock the furniture was inside the house and the farmer had started back to Cedarton.

"Know something, Kay?" Danny said, mopping the perspiration from his forehead. "I don't care what anybody tells you. This moving is rugged."

"You can't get tired now, Danny. There's too much to do."

"We'd better stop for the night." Danny pulled her down beside him on the sofa. "We can't take a chance of having you get too tired."

"I've never felt better," she protested, smiling. "Are you sure you're concerned about me, or are you worrying about yourself?"

"I'll never tell."

Nevertheless, they stopped working, fixed supper, and waited until morning to start again. By the next evening they had the furniture arranged and rearranged, the curtains up, and the boxes of dishes unpacked.

"Now," Kay exclaimed, stretching luxuriously and surveying the neat little room, "we're ready to start living."

Danny picked up the morning paper and opened it carelessly. "I saw the boy next door a little while ago."

Kay brightened.

"Did you have a chance to talk to him?"

"For a couple of minutes."

Danny put aside the paper.

"He's interested in hot rods. In fact, he challenged me to a drag race, giving me a head start because I've got such an old car."

"And when does this big event take place?" Kay asked, her eyes dancing.

"I told him you did all the racing in our family."

"You didn't!" she protested indignantly.

"He said he was coming over to talk to you."

"Danny!"

"Well, you wanted to get acquainted with him and his sister, didn't you?"

"Not that way."

"Now what's wrong with meeting them that way," Danny demanded, "as long as you meet them?"

"You're teasing me, aren't you?" Kay asked seriously.

"Maybe a little," he confessed. "I did talk with Brad Wheeler and kidded around with him. But to tell you the truth, I couldn't tell whether he was laughing with me or at me."

The smile left Kay's face.

"What's he like, Danny? Were you able to get acquainted with him? I mean, do you think you made friends with him?"

"That's something I couldn't tell. He seemed cordial enough, but like so many high-school kids, he seemed to have a shell around him. I got to know him I thought, but after he left, I suddenly realized that I didn't get to know him at all."

Kay pushed her hair back into place and for a moment or two said nothing.

"I can tell you this much," Danny went on, "neither he nor his sister know anything at all about the Gospel. They're as pagan as any two Indians in the jungles of Guatemala."

"It's a real challenge to us, Danny. It's something to have an opportunity to witness like that while we're here."

"That's right. It certainly gives our living here in Pawhasset real purpose."

"Wouldn't it be marvelous if we could win them for Christ before we go back to the field?"

Early the following week, Tex Williams flew up to Pawhasset and took Danny and Kay to the Angle.

"I know you won't have time to do everything you want to do up there," the gray-haired pilot said, "but you'll have a chance to look around and get a good start on the job. And when we come back next time, maybe you'll be able to finish."

They got into the plane and Danny got behind the controls. He took off smoothly, circled the little airfield, and headed out across the Big Traverse on the Lake of the Woods.

"Nice job, Danny," Tex said admiringly. "You handle a plane like a veteran. You've got a real flair for flying."

"I certainly love it, if that means anything."

"It's not going to be long until you'll be able to fly anywhere that I do," Tex said. He smiled. "Seeing you fly this way makes me wish I could keep you up here. I'll be needing a new pilot if my plans work out."

"Don't tell me you're going to retire."

"Not exactly. I may not try to get the contract to fly mail into the Angle again. I've about decided to start a flying school at Baudette and go out after more freelance bush flying. The mines in Canada are pleading with me to do it. But if I do, I'll have to get a new plane and either take in a partner or hire a good bush pilot. Neither one is going to be easy to do."

Danny smiled.

"If we weren't going back to Guatemala, I'd sure be interested. I don't know of anyone I'd rather work with than you, Tex."

"And I don't know anyone I'd rather work with than you, Danny."

"Of course, I couldn't consider anything like that, Tex. As soon as the doctor gives Kay the word that she's all right we'll be heading for Guatemala."

"I know that," the pilot replied. "I was just thinking out loud."

CHAPTER 11

A REAL BLOW

The last day of school at Cedarton was approaching rapidly, and the Orlis family had everything packed and ready to go back to the Angle.

"It sure is going to be great to get home again," Jim Morgan said to Ron Orlis as the two of them carried a small trunk from one of the upstairs rooms to the lower hall. "I just can't wait to get back there and go fishing again. Remember all the walleyes you and I got early last summer?"

Ron grinned. "We had so many that Mom made us give some away."

Jim nodded.

"You're a lucky stiff to be getting back there now," Ron told him. "You'll be home a couple of weeks before Roxie and I are able to make it."

"It's going to be great to get back, that's for sure.

But there's an awful lot of work to do. I might not even do any fishing before you get there."

"If I know you," Ron told him, "you'll get out fishing somehow. And I don't blame you. I'd sure do the same thing if I had the chance."

At the bottom of the stairs they paused, breathing heavily.

"It's going to be nice to have Danny and Kay around, isn't it?" Jim commented.

"That's one thing that is really going to be extra special this year. It's been a long time since I've gone fishing with Danny. You'll learn more fishing with him in one day than you will fishing with anyone else for a month, except Dad."

During the next few days, the weather was good and Tex Williams had a great deal of flying to do. He spent most of his airtime in the right seat of the Cessna with Danny at the controls, while he noted his procedures carefully, step by step. Tex checked Danny out on floats as soon as he felt he was ready, and taught him how to make simple engine repairs.

"When you're forced down up here," he explained, "you're really on your own. Knowing how to make some of these repairs and adjustments can save you a long walk or worse."

"I've been doing some tinkering with radio at home too," Danny said. "I used to do some of that as a kid, you know, when I had a two-way radio. Radio can make the difference in Guatemala too."

"It can make the difference up here too," Tex replied.

With the intensive flying they were doing, takeoffs and landings, even on floats, became routine. Once that was accomplished, Danny was able to turn his attention to navigation and cross-country flying.

"We use maps and charts, of course," Tex explained, "but most of our flying is done by dead reckoning. We keep contact with the ground and fly from one landmark to another, the same as you would find your way through the woods on the ground."

"I've been trying to use charts, Tex," Danny said, "but I don't feel at ease unless I've got a hill or a stream or a funny-shaped lake or pond to go by."

Tex Williams nodded approvingly.

"You're going to do all right, Danny. You've got the natural instincts of a bush pilot."

"It grows on a guy," Danny said thoughtfully.

"After a while you get to the place where you believe you can even think better in the air," the pilot remarked.

* * *

Kay had been trying to get acquainted with Brad Wheeler and his sister who lived next door but had little success. In fact, it seemed impossible.

"I've tried and tried to talk to them, Danny," she said, "but they almost run when I start their way."

"I haven't gotten very far with them either. I've

had a chance to talk to Brad a couple of times, but Connie acts as though I'm not even around."

"Do you suppose they know we're Christians?" Kay wondered.

"I'm sure they do. Brad was friendly enough the first time I talked with him. Ever since, he's acted as though I had the plague."

"But he will talk to you," Kay went on. "At least that's something. It's more than I have been able to do."

Danny got a glass from the cupboard and filled it with milk.

"He talks to me all right, but he always acts as though he's in a terrific hurry. I've never had a good chance to do any serious talking with him."

Kay pulled out a chair and sat at the table across from him.

"Do you think it would do any good to invite Connie over?" she asked. "Do you think she would come?"

"There's one way of finding out."

"I think I'll do it," she said, "as soon as we get back from Cedarton."

"Back from Cedarton?" Danny echoed. "I didn't even know we were going."

"I'm supposed to go back to the doctor for a checkup. You haven't forgotten that, have you?"

He glanced at the calendar with the date circled with black crayon.

"I had forgotten until right now. But I guess it is time to go down and see Doc at that."

They made arrangements to borrow one of Tex Williams' planes and flew down to Cedarton the following morning to keep Kay's appointment with the doctor.

"Do you want me to go with you while you see him, Kay?"

"You can if you want to," she said, "but I don't think there's any need for it. I'm getting along fine. All I'm hoping is that he'll say I'm ready to go back to Guatemala."

"Now we're not going to be in any hurry about that. An extra month or two isn't going to make any difference as long as you get all right."

"I know that, Danny. But I can't help getting concerned about it. I even wake up in the middle of the night thinking about Guatemala and wondering when we will go back. There's so much to be done for the Lord out there and so few are concerned enough to help."

"You don't have to sell me on the idea of going back, Kay. I'm as intent on getting out to the field as you are. But I just want to be sure that you are all right. That's my big concern."

"I'm all right now."

At the door to the doctor's office, they parted.

"I'm going over to visit Harold Forester," Danny said. "You can phone me there or stop by when you've finished."

Kay went into the doctor's office. He was not particularly busy that afternoon and was able to see her almost immediately. He finished his examination and made a few notes on her chart. She watched him with growing tenseness.

"How have you been, Mrs. Orlis?"

"I've been feeling fine," she told him. "As well as I've ever felt."

He nodded.

"You seem to be doing very well. In fact, you've been doing much better than I had expected."

"You don't know how happy that makes me. It's a real answer to prayer."

"I don't think it will be necessary for you to come back and see me unless you start feeling worse again. And I don't think that's likely."

Kay got to her feet.

"You don't know how much that news means to me and my husband. We can scarcely wait to get back to Guatemala."

The doctor looked at her, scowling. He scribbled on the chart and did not speak.

"What did you say about Guatemala?" he asked sternly.

"I said we could hardly wait to get back to our mission station. There's so much work to be done out there, and they're so very short of workers."

"I have no doubt of that," he answered. "But to be very frank with you, someone else is going to have to do it."

"What do you mean?"

"I mean you're not going back to Guatemala or to any other country in the tropics," he said slowly. "You'd just as well forget it!"

CHAPTER 12

"FORGET IT"

Kay stared at the doctor in disbelief. Perspiration came out on her forehead and moistened her trembling hands. Her head spun.

Not go back to Guatemala? That couldn't be true. She didn't hear him correctly. Either that or he was joking. Hadn't he just said she was all right? That she didn't even have to see him again?

"But, doctor," she persisted, "we've got to go back to Guatemala. We're needed out there. That's where the Lord had called us to serve Him!"

The doctor closed her chart with a snap and turned to face her. When he spoke, his voice was harsh and cold.

"Young woman, I don't presume to understand you religious people with your so-called 'calls from, the Lord.' But I am a doctor and I understand my profession." He reached over and took a big medical book from his desk. "I know that anyone who has suffered heat exhaustion and has been as close to heat stroke as you have been will never be able to take the terrific heat of the tropics. You'd just as well forget it!"

"But I feel wonderful, doctor," Kay persisted. "I feel as good as I did before I–I got sick."

"You probably do. And we want you to stay that way."

Kay caught her breath. She swayed slightly and grasped the desk for support.

"This is something you're going to have to accept, Mrs. Orlis, whether you want to or not." His voice was stern. "You feel fine now, and the chances are you'll continue to feel that way as long as you stay in a temperate climate."

His eyes softened a little and he got to his feet. It was obvious that he had found his task distasteful.

"I know how much this means to you, but there is no use in deceiving you by holding out false hope. Your days in the tropics are over. Finished. You've destroyed the tolerance your body had for prolonged heat. You will never be able to go back into the tropics and stay for any length of time. In fact, you're fortunate to be alive."

He did mean what he said. That realization seeped slowly through Kay's consciousness. He didn't want to have to tell her the truth, but there was nothing else to do. Suddenly the strength was gone from her body and all their dreams for the future vanished.

"I–I don't know what to say," Kay stammered. "This is one thing neither Danny nor I have ever seriously considered. We've always figured our stay in the States was temporary. We've been counting the days until we could go back."

The doctor shook his head.

"I'll never be able to understand people like you and your husband," he said. "I can't see why you would want to change anyone's religion in the first place. But if you feel you've got to meddle in other people's lives, there should be enough to work on in this country without going to a miserable place like Guatemala."

"But it's not miserable," she answered. "It's the most wonderful place I've ever been. And those people need help so desperately. You can't realize it until you've been out there and have seen them."

He spoke gruffly.

"Maybe so. But somebody else is going to have to do your job. You're through down there. And the sooner you realize it the better."

Kay stumbled out of his office to the outer desk where she stopped and paid her bill.

"Will you be making another appointment?" the receptionist asked.

Kay heard her voice dimly, as though she were far, far away. For a moment she didn't realize what the receptionist had said.

She repeated her question.

"I beg your pardon!" Kay exclaimed.

"Did the doctor ask you to see him again? If he did, we can make your appointment now."

"No," Kay said. "No, there won't be any more appointments. I won't be coming back anymore."

The receptionist stared at her quizzically.

Kay made her way out into the warm afternoon sunshine.

"Hello, Kay," a familiar voice said as she stepped out on the sidewalk, but she neither saw nor heard her friend. She went on down the street, not even realizing that anyone had spoken to her.

The doctor's words coursed through her mind in an endless, mocking refrain.

"You'll never go back to Guatemala! You'll never go back to Guatemala! You had just as well forget it! You'll never go back!"

The doctor had said he didn't understand Christians or how their minds worked. He acted as though he hated those who did believe. He must have gotten a real thrill just now, blasting her dreams and hopes.

Kay's cheeks went hot, and instantly her body stiffened with anger. Something close to hatred blazed within her. Hatred for the doctor, for the entire medical profession.

It wouldn't hurt her to go back. He was just being perverse. He wanted to keep her and Danny from Guatemala. That was it!

But she was being unfair, she realized. The doctor was not able to understand Christians, but he was a kind man. He had taken no particular pleasure in crushing her. He was speaking only as a physician and had said only what he felt he had to say.

But that scarcely made it any easier.

She and Danny weren't going back to their little tropical home on the mission compound ever. They would never again see those kind, trusting Christian nationals who had believed them when they promised to come back. What would the Indians think when she and Danny did not return? How could they possibly understand?

At last Kay was able to move again. She crossed the street and went down a narrow, tree-lined walk without thought of where she was going. She couldn't see Danny. Not yet. Not until she had better control of herself. Not until she could push back the tears enough to keep from crying.

"Oh, God!" her tortured heart cried. "Why? Why?"

But there was no answer. She continued to walk blindly up one block, across the street, and down the other.

At last, she returned to the business district and headed toward Mr. Forester's office. Danny met her at a street corner half a block away.

"Where have you been, Kay?" he cried, hurrying up to her. "I've been looking all over for you."

"I–I'm sorry, Danny," was all she could manage. "I'm terribly sorry."

The ache in her heart grew quickly until it almost overwhelmed her. She fought to keep her lower lip from trembling.

Danny saw the hurt in her face, the bewilderment, the pain in her eyes.

"What's wrong, Kay? What did the doctor say?"

Her shoulders twitched convulsively.

"What did he tell you? Aren't you getting along all right?"

She nodded.

"Then what is it?" he demanded.

It was a long while before Kay could speak.

"The doctor said that we – I mean, he said that I won't be able to go back to Guatemala again. Ever!"

Danny recoiled suddenly, as though her words were a lash.

"Are–are you sure?"

She nodded.

"But it can't be true, Danny! It can't be true! We've got to go back! We promised everyone that we would be back as soon as–as soon as–"

Her voice broke.

"Of course, it isn't true," Danny told her. "God has called us to serve Him in Guatemala. That's where our life is. He'll see that we get back. We can be sure of that."

He would have said more, but somehow words seemed futile, so out of place.

"That's exactly what I tried to tell the doctor, Danny. But he–he wouldn't listen."

Kay felt better already, just having Danny with her. She seemed to draw strength from his firm, strong hand, from the tone of his voice, from his very presence at her side.

As they walked back to Mr. Forester's office, Danny spoke softly.

"I knew something was wrong when you were gone so long. I was terribly concerned about you, so I went out to look for you."

"I–I'm sorry, Danny. I didn't even think of that. All I could think of was our work on the field, and how much we're needed out there. And what it means to you – to us."

"It doesn't mean any more to me than it does to you, Kay," he said. "God called us both to serve Him down there."

They paused before Mr. Forester's office.

"Are you going to tell him what the doctor told us?" she asked.

"We need his prayers."

Mr. Forester listened understandingly as Kay told him all that had taken place. He sat there quietly; hands folded on his desk.

There was little to say. Yet, even before they finished talking, they felt the comfort and strength of understanding, Christian fellowship and love.

Finally, Mr. Forester spoke. His voice was soft and gentle.

"This is one of those things that is difficult to understand. Just as it was difficult for us to understand how the transverse myelitis that struck Marilyn could possibly have been His will. But we know He watches over us and takes care of us, and whatever happens to those who trust Him is a part of His purpose and plan. We have to trust Him."

"But how could this be a part of His plan?" Kay asked, struggling to fathom what he was saying. "There are thousands of people out in our part of Guatemala who are lost because no one has gone to tell them of Christ."

Her voice choked, and it was a moment or two before she could go on.

"And the worst of it is that so few seem to care."

She breathed deeply, and then finished.

"I think I would feel differently about not going back if I knew there was someone to take our place. But there isn't, Mr. Forester! It seems that no one listens to God's call to the mission field anymore! No one wants to go and tell our people of Jesus!"

CHAPTER 13

ANOTHER MISSION FIELD

Danny and Kay sat in Mr. Forester's office for half an hour or so.

"If I were you," Mr. Forester counselled, "I would contact the mission doctor as quickly as possible and get his opinion about your condition and the possibility of your going back to the field. After all, he's the one you will look to for a decision."

Danny glanced at Kay, who by this time was sitting tense and quiet, listening.

"That's something I never thought of," Danny said. "Would you like to go down to Minneapolis and have Dr. Frazer examine you before we go back home?"

Her voice trembled slightly.

"If you think it's best, Danny."

Danny called Dr. Frazer from Mr. Forester's private office and made an appointment to see him the following morning.

"I'll take you out to the airport whenever you're ready," Harold Forester told him.

Before leaving his office they all bowed their heads in prayer. When they finished Mr. Forester turned to Kay.

"I want you to know that Carrie and I will be remembering you."

"Thank you," Kay said softly.

They left Mr. Forester's car at the airport and started across the drive to the little building that served the local manager as an office.

"I want to see Dr. Frazer and all of that," she confided. "In fact, I know I won't be satisfied until we've been down to see him. But, Danny, I–I'm afraid to talk to him. I'm afraid of what he might tell us."

Danny looked at her reassuringly.

"Dr. Frazer has been a missionary himself. He's as interested in the field as we are. He'll understand."

They flew down to Minneapolis that afternoon, stayed in a hotel uptown, and the following morning went to see the mission doctor. He ushered them into his private office and closed the door.

"Now," he began, looking from one to the other, "what seems to be the trouble?"

"I think you probably have more information than we do, doctor," Danny said. "You've received a copy of the medical report on Kay's heat exhaustion in Guatemala, haven't you?"

Dr. Frazer nodded.

"I was studying it when you came in. Thought probably I should go over it again after you phoned yesterday."

He paused.

"Why did you wish to see me, Mrs. Orlis? Have you been having more trouble?"

"Oh, no," she answered. "I've been feeling fine. In fact, I think I feel as well as I ever have – even before I got sick."

"Now that is encouraging. You are a very fortunate young woman. I'm sure your doctor has already told you that you were on the brink of a heat stroke. Actually, you could have been within a half hour of having a heat stroke when the nurse got you in the shade and set to work. It was that close."

Danny shuddered.

"Heat stroke is a frightening thing," the doctor went on. "Humanly speaking, there is little chance of recovery for a person who has one. That's why it really thrills me to see you."

"We've been thinking so much about the work back in Guatemala, Dr. Frazer," Danny said. "They're so short-handed out there, and things were going so well for us. We've been wondering about going back."

The doctor's eyes clouded.

"We haven't given it much thought until lately," Danny added, "but Kay has been feeling so well we thought it might be possible to go back soon."

"Did you mention this to your doctor in Cedarton?" the doctor asked.

"I saw him yesterday," Kay answered. "He wasn't very encouraging. He–"

She tried but could not continue.

"He isn't a Christian, Dr. Frazer," Danny explained, "and he doesn't understand why we would want to go to Guatemala in the first place. We thought perhaps he was letting his prejudice color his opinion."

"I've talked with the mission's general secretary about you two," the doctor said. "Mr. Dalton has been planning on stopping by to see you the first time he's in your area."

Neither Danny nor Kay could bring themselves to speak.

"You know," the doctor went on, choosing his words carefully, "this is the sort of thing that makes my job difficult."

A hurt, bewildered look flickered in Kay's eyes.

"Do you mean we won't be able to go back?" Danny asked, putting into words the question Kay could not bring herself to ask.

The doctor nodded.

"I'm awfully sorry to have to tell you that. Believe me, I am. But there are times when God leads us in mysterious ways. Ways we find impossible to understand. That is what has happened in your case. We can't understand. All we can do is trust that God in His wisdom is doing what is best for us."

"But we both have such a burden for Guatemala," Kay protested miserably. "It's all we can think about.

And before we left, we promised the people that we would be back."

"They'll understand."

The doctor smiled to soften the import of his words.

"You will be all right, Mrs. Orlis, as long as you stay in a temperate zone. You'll feel as good as you ever did and never know that you've been ill. The strange thing is that that doesn't change the situation. You have lost your capacity to withstand the rigors of heat. You couldn't possibly go back into the tropics and carry on."

The hurt in Kay's heart was reflected in her face. She looked as though she would never smile again.

"But why?" she asked simply. "Why would God call Danny and me to Guatemala as missionaries and then permit something like this to happen?"

Dr. Frazer took his time in answering.

"Who can say why God does or does not do anything?" he asked. "It is only ours to trust. It maybe that your stay in Guatemala was only a preparation for the real work God is calling you to do; a testing for a work that He wants you in."

At the moment Kay's hurt was too deep to understand what he had said.

Danny and Kay left his office presently and went back to the airport. Kay sat quietly in the cab, her face taut and drawn. Danny struggled for words, but there were none to comfort her.

"It doesn't seem real, Danny," Kay finally said. "It

can't be real. Our call to Guatemala was so clear – so direct. We couldn't have been mistaken in it, could we?"

Danny felt the ache in his own heart, but he forced it aside.

"God called us to Guatemala, Kay," he told her. "We couldn't have been mistaken about that. But He has a purpose in everything that He does, or permits to happen. It might be as the doctor said. Guatemala could just be a preparation for us. Perhaps He called us down there to give us a real burden for all who are outside of Christ. Now that we have that burden He may be getting ready to call us to the work He wants us to spend our lives doing."

Kay thought about that for a moment in silence.

"I suppose you could be right," she answered. There was doubt in her voice. "But it seems so strange that we would be so happy there, that we would feel so completely in the center of His will if it was only a preparation for something else."

Danny searched in vain for words. The desperation in her voice echoed in his own heart. They had been happy in Guatemala. Happier than they had ever been in their lives before. Why was that if the call wasn't permanent? Why?

Kay gave voice to the words.

"Danny, why would God do this?" she asked. There was no self-pity in her voice. Only concern.

He took her hand in his.

"It may be that we'll know the answer to that

question in a very short time. Or we may not know it as long as we live. But we can be sure of this. All that God does is right. And the most important thing for you and me is to be in the center of His will. We can't think of our own wishes. We can't complain because things don't work out as we want them to."

"I know all of that, Danny. We'll have to pray to be willing to accept it."

She took a deep breath.

"It would be so different if there were plenty of young people to go out to the mission field," she went on as though to herself. "If there was just someone who would take our place, Danny, I could understand it. I think I could take it a great deal easier. But there's no one to go! There are people dying without the Savior, and there is no one to tell them of Him!"

"We've got to leave that in God's hands, Kay. He knows. He loves them more than we do."

They went to the plane and Danny flew directly back to Pawhasset. Their car was still sitting at the airport.

"It won't be long until we'll be home," Danny said, getting into the old car and starting the engine.

Kay shivered.

When they pulled up to their little bungalow, the same group of youngsters who had been there when they came to look at the house were gathered in the driveway beside the house next door.

"I tell you it won't start," Brad said angrily. "We've got to call a mechanic."

"Who's got money enough for that?"

Danny turned to Kay.

"Come on, honey."

They went over to the place where the kids were standing around an old car.

"Got troubles?" Danny asked.

"Troubles?" Brad echoed. "I'll say we've got troubles."

One of the other boys started to swear, but Brad stopped him.

"Don't do that. This guy's a preacher."

"Missionary," Danny corrected, moving next to the car. "Have you checked the automatic choke?"

"That can't be it!"

"Hurry up!" a girl said. "I'm getting cold."

"Why don't you come in," Kay suggested. "You can get warm and we can make some hot chocolate while you're waiting. I'll get the groceries out of our car.

They looked at her suspiciously but followed her into the house.

Although they had been gone for two days the oil barrel had been full and the house was warm. The girls gathered around the heater while Kay went into the kitchen. By the time she served the hot drink, the girls were visiting with her in a friendly way.

"I think they've got the old jalopy going," one of them said.

"I'm not leaving until I've finished this hot chocolate," another replied. "I didn't realize how hungry I was.

That was the opening Kay had been waiting for.

"I have an idea," she said. "Why don't you go out and ask the guys to come in for a chili feed in about a half hour?"

As soon as Danny got the car running, he went back to the store. The guys and girls called their parents and it wasn't long until all six of them and Danny and Kay were sitting around the table eating and talking gaily.

One of the boys pulled out a cigarette when he finished eating, but the guy next to him poked him sharply in the ribs.

"Don't be a sap!"

It was almost 9 o'clock before they left.

"Boy," Brad said warmly, "we sure didn't figure on this. Here we had our car busted down. You fixed it and gave us a feed beside."

"And," his sister added warmly as she held out her hand to Kay, "we had a wonderful time!"

"You're welcome to come over any time."

"We'll be here," they said. "You can count on that."

Danny and Kay stood in the doorway together, waving goodbye to their guests. The kids didn't see the tears in their eyes.

"Danny," Kay cried, her voice choking, "it's happened! We've made friends with them! I'm so happy I could cry!"

"I was thinking something else," he said thoughtfully. "We've been wondering why God doesn't permit us to go back to the mission field. *We're already there, Kay!* Kids are our mission field! Those who don't know Christ right here at home!"

Kay nodded.

Tears were coursing down her cheeks unashamedly. Tears of praise, thanksgiving, and happiness.

THE DANNY ORLIS SERIES

The Danny Orlis series, by Bernard Palmer, delivers a blend of adventure, mystery, and suspense through various settings—from the Canadian wilderness to Guatemalan jungles. Danny Orlis, an adept outdoorsman, skilled athlete, and committed Christian, employs his quick thinking, calm bravery, and biblical solutions to confront everyday problems and hair-raising dangers. Early stories focus on Danny navigating school life, sports, and outdoor challenges, while in later books, Danny and his wife Kay provide wisdom and guidance to youngsters facing lifelike situations and challenges. Having sold over two million copies, this series has made Palmer a renowned author in Christian youth literature. Palmer is also the author of the Felicia Cartright series and various other series for Christian youth.

AVAILABLE FROM WWW.ANEKOPRESS.COM

www.ingramcontent.com/pod-product-compliance
Lightning Source LLC
Chambersburg PA
CBHW070911100726
47907CB00008B/2281